PENGUIN BOOKS

WRITERS FROM THE OTHER EUROPE
General Editor: Philip Roth

THIS WAY FOR THE GAS, LADIES AND GENTLEMEN

Tadeusz Borowski was born in the Ukraine in 1922. Having survived Auschwitz and Dachau, he died by his own hand in Warsaw in 1951. His life, which epitomizes "the historical destiny of man," is recounted in Jan Kott's Introduction to this volume.

Born in Poland in 1914, Jan Kott studied at the University of Warsaw and at the Sorbonne. During World War II he fought with the Polish Army, took part in the resistance to the Nazis, edited an underground weekly, and served in the Polish People's Army. He taught for many years at the University of Warsaw and, having come to the United States in 1966, is currently professor of English and comparative literature at the State University of New York at Stony Brook. Books by him include *Shakespeare Our Contemporary*, *Theatre Notebook*, and *The Eating of the Gods*.

TADEUSZ BOROWSKI

THIS WAY FOR THE GAS, LADIES AND GENTLEMEN

Selected and translated by Barbara Vedder

Introduction by Jan Kott
Introduction translated by Michael Kandel

Penguin Books

PENGUIN BOOKS
Published by the Penguin Group
Viking Penguin, a division of Penguin Books USA Inc.,
375 Hudson Street, New York, New York 10014, U.S.A.
Penguin Books Ltd, 27 Wrights Lane, London W8 5TZ, England
Penguin Books Australia Ltd, Ringwood, Victoria, Australia
Penguin Books Canada Ltd, 2801 John Street,
Markham, Ontario, Canada L3R 1B4
Penguin Books (N.Z.) Ltd, 182–190 Wairau Road, Auckland 10, New Zealand

Penguin Books Ltd, Registered Offices:
Harmondsworth, Middlesex, England

Originally published in *Wybor Opowiadan*,
Pantswowy Instytyt Wydawniczy, Poland, 1959
First published in the United States of America by
Viking Penguin Inc. 1967
Published in Penguin Books 1976

17   19   20   18

ISBN 0 14 00.4114 1

Printed in the United States of America

WRITERS FROM THE OTHER EUROPE

The purpose of this paperback series is to bring together outstanding and influential works of fiction by Eastern European writers. In many instances they will be writers who, though recognized as powerful forces in their own cultures, are virtually unknown in the West. It is hoped that by reprinting selected Eastern European writers in this format and with introductions that place each work in its literary and historical context, the literature that has evolved in "the other Europe," particularly during the postwar decades, will be made more accessible to a new readership.

PHILIP ROTH

OTHER TITLES IN THIS SERIES

*Ashes and Diamonds**
by Jerzy Andrzejewski
Introduction by Heinrich Böll

The Book of Laughter and Forgetting
by Milan Kundera
Afterword: A Talk with the Author by Philip Roth

Closely Watched Trains
by Bohumil Hrabal
Introduction by Josef Škvorecký

The Farewell Party
by Milan Kundera
Introduction by Elizabeth Pochoda

*Laughable Loves**
by Milan Kundera
Introduction by Philip Roth

Opium and Other Stories
by Géza Csáth
Introduction by Angela Carter

Sanatorium under the Sign of the Hourglass
by Bruno Schulz
Introduction by John Updike

The Street of Crocodiles
by Bruno Schulz
Introduction by Jerzy Ficowski

*A Tomb for Boris Davidovich**
by Danilo Kiš
Introduction by Joseph Brodsky

*Available in Great Britain

Contents

Translator's Note

This selection from the work of Tadeusz Borowski is intentionally limited to the stories inspired by his concentration-camp experiences. Borowski, who was born in 1922, was imprisoned in Auschwitz and Dachau from 1943 to 1945. The first collection of his concentration-camp stories was written in collaboration with two friends and published in Munich in 1946. Two others, which contain his best work and from which the present selection is drawn, appeared in Poland in 1948. They are *Pozegnanie z Maria* (Farewell to Maria) and *Kamienny Swiat* (A World of Stone). His very first book, a volume of poetry *Gdziekolwiek Ziemia* (Wherever the Earth), appeared as an underground publication in 1942 during the German occupation of Poland. Another volume of his poetry, *Imiona Nurtu* (The Names of Currents) was published in 1945. Most of Borowski's later work, after his return to Poland, belongs to political journalism. He committed suicide in Warsaw in 1951. His Collected Works, published posthumously in 1954, comprise five volumes.

Borowski's work attracted much attention, and his stories of the camps were highly acclaimed in Polish literary circles. Despite the deceptive simplicity of his style and his documentary technique, his writing carries a burden of meaning that far transcends the merely actual.

Introduction

Tadeusz Borowski opened a gas valve on July 1, 1951.
He was not yet thirty. Borowski's suicide was a shock that
one can compare only to the suicide, twenty-one years
before, of Vladimir Mayakovski. Borowski was the greatest hope of Polish literature among the generation of
his contemporaries decimated by the war. He was also the
greatest hope of the Communist party, as well as its apostle
and inquisitor; many years had to pass before many of
us realized that he was also its martyr. The five-volume
posthumous edition of his collected works contains poetry,
journalistic writings, news articles, novels, and short
stories; among the latter are at least a hundred pages
published by a boy of twenty-four one year after his re-
lease from the concentration camps at Dachau and
Auschwitz, pages that—as was written after Borowski's
death—"will very likely last as long as Polish literature
exists." Borowski's Auschwitz stories, however, are not only
a masterpiece of Polish—and of world—literature. Among
the tens of thousands of pages written about the holocaust
and the death camps, Borowski's slender book continues

to occupy, for more than a quarter century now, a place apart. The book is one of the cruelest of testimonies to what men did to men, and a pitiless verdict that anything can be done to a human being.

Borowski also left behind the story of his life. There are lives of writers which not only belong to the history of literature but are also literature themselves—that is, human destiny epitomized. These are primarily the biographies of poets who abandoned literature like Arthur Rimbaud, who fell into madness like Friedrich Hölderlin, or who committed suicide like Heinrich von Kleist and Sylvia Plath. The existential experience is contained in those life stories; the boundaries where literature ends and the realm of silence begins are revealed. Borowski's biography is different. It reveals what I would call the historical destiny of man. Romain Gary, a French writer of Polish origin who spent his childhood in Vilna, called his first novel, about the years of the German occupation, *Une Éducation Européenne.* There are years and places, sometimes whole decades and entire nations, in which history reveals its menace and destructive force with particular clarity. These are *chosen* nations, in the same sense in which the Bible calls the Jews a *chosen* people. In such places and years history is—as my teacher used to say—"let off the leash." It is then that individual human destiny seems as if shaped directly by history, becoming only a chapter in it.

Borowski received a full "European education." One might even say overeducation. He was born in 1922 in Zhitomir, in the Soviet Ukraine, to Polish parents. His father, a bookkeeper, was transported in 1926 to Karelia, above the Arctic Circle, to dig the famous White Sea Canal. That was one of the harshest labor camps. He was exiled for his participation in a Polish military organization during World War I. When Tadeusz was eight, his mother was in turn sent to a settlement a little nearer, on the Yenisei River, in Siberia. Those were the years of collectivization and hunger. The monthly food allowance amounted to two pounds of flour. During this time young Tadeusz was taken care of by his aunt; he went to school and tended cows.

In 1932 the elder Borowski was exchanged for Communists imprisoned in Poland, and Tadeusz was repatriated by the Red Cross. His mother joined the family in Warsaw two years later. The father worked in a warehouse, and the mother made a little money sewing dresses at home; life was difficult. They put their son in a boarding school run by Franciscan monks, where he could study for next to nothing. When the war began, he was not yet seventeen. During the German occupation secondary school and college were forbidden to Poles. Borowski studied in underground classes. In the spring of 1940 the first big roundups began in Warsaw. He was just then taking his final examinations. That day is described in his "Graduation on Market Street": "A long column of automobiles stationed itself at the end of the avenue and waited for streetcars like a tiger tracking antelope. We spilled out of the moving trolley like pears and tore diagonally across a field newly planted with vegetables. The earth smelled of spring. . . . And in the city, on the other side of the river, as in a deep jungle, people were being hunted." This final exam during the roundup was a "European" certificate of maturity.

Borowski obtained a job as a night watchman and stockboy in a firm that sold building materials. At that time, of course, young people worked mainly in order to have a work card, which kept them from being shipped off to the Reich. One made one's actual living through illegal or semilegal trade. Building materials were hard to come by; on the black market they were sold for ten times more than the regulated prices. Borowski tried to make ends meet and studied literature in underground university courses. The lectures took place in private apartments and, for safety, in small groups. Of the group of thirteen to which he belonged, five are not alive today.

He began writing early. In a seminar on English literature he drew attention with his translation of the fool's songs from Shakespeare's *Twelfth Night.* He wrote, of course, his own poems too. He published them in the winter of 1942, in an edition of 165 copies.

With the exception of the official collaborationist daily newspaper and a couple of semipornographic weeklies, not a single Polish periodical appeared legally in German-occupied Poland. Yet in Warsaw alone there appeared each day several dozen underground leaflets and war bulletins transcribed from radio stations in the West. Political periodicals of every orientation came out. "Censorship" did not exist—the printing, distribution, and even possession of such underground literature was punishable by death or, at the very least, the concentration camp. As never before and as never again, Warsaw under Hitler's occupation was a city of the clandestine press. The periodicals were not only from political parties and military groups; a club of mountain climbers published its own underground yearbook, and chess players put out an underground monthly devoted to end games.

There were also underground editions of poetry. Borowski ran off his first volume of poetry himself on a mimeograph, which—he was to recollect afterward with irony in a postwar story—"while used to run off extremely precious radio bulletins and good advice (along with diagrams) on how to conduct street battles in the larger cities, served also to print up lofty, metaphysical hexameters." His volume, *Wherever the Earth,* predicted in classical cadences the extermination of mankind. Its dominant image was that of a gigantic labor camp. Already, in that first volume of poetry, there was no hope, no comfort, no pity. The last poem, "A Song," concluded with a prophecy delivered like a sentence: "We'll leave behind us iron scrap/ and the hollow, mocking laugh of generations."

A few weeks later Borowski was arrested. His fiancée, with whom he was living, had not returned for the night. She had fallen into a trap set by the Nazis at the apartment of some mutual friends. The following day Borowski began searching the city for her. He ended up at that very same apartment—and that very same trap. He had with him his poems and Aldous Huxley's *Brave New World*.

He sat in prison a little over two months. The prison was on the border of the Warsaw ghetto. From the cell window he could see soldiers throwing grenades at the tenements and systematically setting fire to one house after another along the opposite side of the street. At the end of April he was sent with a transport of prisoners to Auschwitz. On his arm they tattooed the camp serial number 119 198. His fiancée was brought to the camp in another transport. They were both "lucky." Three weeks earlier "Aryans" had stopped being sent to the gas chambers—except for special cases. From then on only Jews were gassed en masse.

At first he worked carrying telegraph poles. Then he wound up in the camp hospital with pneumonia. "A True Story," included in this collection, is indeed true. In the hospital he was laid on the same straw mattress on which the "boy with a Bible," Borowski's cellmate at the Warsaw prison, had died of typhoid fever. When Borowski was on his feet again, he was kept at the hospital and given the light work of a night watchman. Then he took a class to become an orderly.

In Auschwitz the third chapter of Borowski's "European education" was acted out, and the second chapter in the history of his love. His fiancée was in the F.K.L. (Frauen Konzentration Lager), the women's barracks, at Birkenau, near Auschwitz. In *Escape from the World of Stone,* a book about Borowski written by Tadeusz Drewnowski, his friend and biographer, the chapter on the stay in Auschwitz bears the title "Tristan 1943." The tale "Auschwitz, Our Home" records the letters sent by the mid-twentieth-century Tristan to his Isolde from the men's to the women's barracks in Auschwitz.

Later Borowski was able to see his fiancée. He was sent to the women's camp to pick up infant corpses. Isolde's head was shaven, and her entire body raw with scabies. Tadeusz was reported to have said: "Don't worry; our children won't be bald." Late in the spring of 1944 he was assigned to a brigade of roofers working in the F.K.L. From then on he saw his fiancée every day. At Auschwitz this was the most dreadful time. The Soviet offensive was approaching, and the Germans stepped up the liquidation of the Jews from the occupied lands. In May and June of 1944 more than four hundred thousand Jews from Hungary were gassed and burned.

In the summer of 1944 the inmates of Auschwitz began to be evacuated into the heart of Germany. Borowski found himself first in a camp outside Stuttgart, then in Dachau. On May 1, 1945, that camp was liberated by the U.S. Seventh Army. The prisoners were transferred to a camp for displaced persons in a former barracks of the S.S. on the outskirts of Monachium. Once again Borowski was behind barbed wire. He left this camp in September and searched desperately for his fiancée. In December he learned from the Red Cross that she had been moved from Birkenau and was alive and living in Sweden. That first year in Europe after the war, however, "the displaced lovers" could not come together across the borders and cordons.

On the land liberated by the Allies there were more than ten million men and women driven from all the German-occupied countries into camps and forced labor, former prisoners of war, and refugees from bombed-out cities. Never before was there such a thin line between the demand for vengeance and the call for justice, between anarchy and law, between the violent need to begin everything anew and the equally desperate need to return to that which was. In those new "Indies in the middle of Europe," as one Polish writer called postwar Germany, young Americans from every state in the Union, from California to Maine, from Nebraska to Texas, had to fill a fourfold function: judges, gendarmes, missionaries, and food suppliers. It was too difficult a task.

Borowski wrote in his Monachium diary at the time: "No doubt the purpose of this whole great war was so that you, friend from Chicago, could cross the salt water, battle your way through all of Germany, and reaching the barbed wire of Allach, share a Camel cigarette with me. . . . And now they've put you on guard duty, to keep an eye on me, and we no longer talk to one another. And I must look like a prisoner to you, for you search me and call me boy. And your slain comrades say nothing."

Europe was divided, right down the middle, into the spheres of influence of the non-Communist Allies and of Russia. Confronting millions of former prisoners of war and refugees was this choice: to remain in exile or to return to the countries in which the Communists had seized power. From Monachium Borowski went for a short while to Murnau, in Bavaria, the headquarters of those Polish soldiers and officers who had decided not to go back. From there he wrote in a letter: "They would give us American pineapples and products of the white man's civilization not seen in Europe for ages: toothbrushes, razor blades, and even chewing gum and powdered eggs, with which we sprinkled our beds, since they were great for keeping off the fleas. . . . All the same I ran from Murnau. I wasn't soldier material—I avoided the meetings, I was no flag-waver, I took to the fields with a stack of books and wandered—the lake in that region is very pretty too."

He went for a short while to Paris, from where he wrote in a letter: "A visitor from a dead, detested country, I plunged into hypocrisy as into the current of a mountain stream. . . . I drank wine with hired women and was even in the Allied Troops Theater, since I am wearing a threadbare uniform, once an English soldier's. I came, I saw—and am sad. . . . A visitor from a dead, detested country, in this place where among shattered homes the girls go walking with Negroes into the eternally reborn vegetation, a poet without listeners and without friends—I don't feel well in Paris." Borowski returned to his country in a repatriation transport on the last day of May 1946. He did not want, as he wrote in one of his last letters from Monachium, "to live with corpses."

For a long time his fiancée did not want to leave Sweden to go to Communist Poland. She returned only in November, after Tadeusz's desperate letters. Borowski rode out to meet her at the border point. "Their first night together, no longer in war but in the liberated homeland," writes Borowski's biographer, "took place behind barbed wire, in the quarantine of a repatriation camp." They were married in December.

Two stories by Borowski, "This Way for the Gas, Ladies and Gentlemen" and "A Day at Harmenz," written back at Monachium as soon as he had been freed, were published in Poland before his arrival. They produced a shock. The public was expecting martyrologies; the Communist party called for works that were ideological, that divided the world into the righteous and the unrighteous, heroes and traitors, Communists and Fascists. Borowski was accused of amorality, decadence, and nihilism. Yet at the same time it was clear to everyone that Polish literature had gained a dazzling new talent. All the publications and all the possibilities the party offered young writers were opened up to Borowski. He was as distrustful as he was ambitious, but he could not resist that most diabolical of temptations —to participate in history, a history for which both stones and people are only the material used to build the "brave new world." At the beginning of 1948 he became a member of the Communist party.

Farewell to Maria, a volume containing his Auschwitz stories, was published around this time, and then the short-story cycle *World of Stone,* about the D.P. camps in Germany and the return to his hometown, where people carry their food and bedding wrapped in bundles from place to place among the ruins like ants. These were the last of Borowski's great stories. After this he wrote stories each week for the Sunday edition of a Warsaw daily which are nothing more than the impassioned journalism of hate. For this, the weakest of his work, he received a government prize. In the summer of 1949 he was sent to Germany to work in the Press Section at the Polish Military Mission in Berlin. The Polish Bureau of Information was located in the Soviet sector of Berlin, the Military Mission in the American sector. These were already the years of the cold war. Borowski found himself at the juncture of two worlds, in a Europe divided down the middle after Yalta.

At that time a few dozen young writers and college graduates in the party traveled from Poland to the East and the West, either to study or to carry out special missions. From Moscow they returned with an incurable ache, depressed and frightened; from the West they returned with smiles and much contempt for decaying capitalism. When Borowski returned to Warsaw after a year in Berlin, it seemed that he no longer had any doubts. In the party they were saying he had "grown into an activist." Literature was supposed to help the party build socialism. Borowski took upon himself the role of taskmaster.

"Literature is not as hard as you think," he wrote. For him literature had become only agitation. "I don't care if they lament my wasting myself on journalism. I don't consider myself a vestal virgin consecrated to prose." It was only to his closest friends that he confided in nightly conversations that—like Mayakovski—he had "stepped on the throat of his own song." I think he was fully aware of the meaning of those words; he had, after all, described many times how the guards in the camps would place a shovel across the neck of a prisoner and jump on it with their boots until he expired. Less than fifteen months after his return from Berlin Borowski committed suicide.

The reasons for suicide are always complex, and Borowski took the mystery of his death with him to the grave. Two attempts at suicide had preceded that final turning on of the gas valve, but at the conclusion of this life history, which is an emblem and a model of the "fate" of Europe, the plot thickens, the threads all tangle, as though spun by the Greek Moirai—the relentless daughters of Inevitability. After his return from Berlin Borowski entered into a liaison with a young girl. Three days before the suicide his wife bore him a daughter. He saw his wife for the last time at the hospital, on the afternoon before the night he killed himself. Thus ended the tale of Tristan and Isolde.

And there is a second thread. A couple of weeks before

the suicide an old friend was arrested, the same friend in whose apartment eight years earlier, in occupied War-saw, Borowski had fallen into the trap set by the Germans while looking for his fiancée. At that time the friend was tortured by the Gestapo; now he was tortured in turn by Polish Security. Borowski interceded with the highest party officials and was told that the people's justice was never mistaken. This was after the denunciation of Tito by Stalin, and the Communists were then hunting down "traitors" with "rightist-nationalistic deviations." Borowski never lived to see his friend's trial.

And there is a third thread. When Borowski left for Berlin, he was entrusted with a special mission, "the kind you don't even tell your wife about"—wrote Borowski's closest friend a few years after his death in a thinly veiled short story. In the years of the cold war, on both sides of the iron curtain, in the name of two different ideolo-gies—yet each considering itself to stand above morality —such missions were accepted more than once by writers and professors, experts on human conscience. The only difference was that in the West "special" missions usually ended with one returning home. "He was successful," continues Borowski's friend in that story à clef, which was clear to everyone, "so when he came home, they gave him a new mission." The title of the story is "Cruel Star." Borowski completed the full course in his "European education." The Moirai, who spin men's fates, have grown mocking in the twentieth century.

Borowski's Auschwitz stories are written in the first person. The narrator of three of the stories is a deputy Kapo, Vorarbeiter Tadeusz. The identification of the au-thor with the narrator was the moral decision of a prisoner who had lived through Auschwitz—an acceptance of mu-tual responsibility, mutual participation, and mutual guilt for the concentration camp. "It is impossible to write about Auschwitz impersonally," Borowski wrote in a review of one of the hagiographic books about the camp. "The first duty of Auschwitzers is to make clear just what a camp is. . . . But let them not forget that the reader will unfailingly ask: But how did it happen that *you* survived? . . . Tell, then, how you bought places in the hospital, easy posts, how you shoved the 'Moslems' [prisoners who had lost the will to live] into the oven, how you bought women, men, what you did in the barracks, unloading the transports, at the gypsy camp; tell about the daily life of the camp, about the hierarchy of fear, about the loneliness of every man. But write that you, you were the ones who did this. That a portion of the sad fame of Auschwitz belongs to you as well."

The four million gassed, led straight from the ramp to the crematoriums, had no choice to make, nor did the prisoners selected for the ovens. In Auschwitz there were individual acts of heroism and a clandestine international military network. Auschwitz has its saint, a Catholic priest who went to an underground cell and a slow death by starvation in order to save the life of an unknown fellow prisoner, but the Auschwitz "of the living," like all the other German camps—and Soviet camps too—was based on the cooperation of the prisoners in the "administering" of terror and death. From the Kapos, who almost without exception were German criminals, to the lowliest functionaries like Vorarbeiter Tadeusz, everyone was assigned a double part: executioner and victim. In *No Exit,* Jean-Paul Sartre's postwar play, the dead in hell are surprised not to see torturers. Hell is organized like a self-service cafeteria. ". . . an economy of man-power or devil-power. The customers serve themselves."

Literature, from the very beginning, recognized this dread identity of executioner and victim. Aeschylus's

Agamemnon, who sacrificed his own daughter on the altar so that the Greek ships could sail to Troy, was murdered by his wife after his victorious return to Greece. Shakespeare's usurpers, in climbing the great staircase of history, murder everyone who stand in their way; at the top of the steps, when they have finally seized the crown, they themselves are murdered by the sons of their victims. In Borowski's Auschwitz stories the difference between executioner and victim is stripped of all greatness and pathos; it is brutally reduced to a second bowl of soup, an extra blanket, or the luxury of a silk shirt and shoes with thick soles, about which Vorarbeiter Tadeusz is so proud.

Auschwitz was not only, as Borowski writes, "the bloodiest battle of the war," but also a gigantic transshipping station, where the plunder from the murdered victims was diverted to the Reich. Scraps of this plunder fell to the privileged prisoners. "Work is not unpleasant," says Vorarbeiter Tadeusz, "when one has eaten a breakfast of smoked bacon with bread and garlic and washed it down with a tin of evaporated milk."

When life is cheap, food and clothing are worth their weight in gold. I was never in a concentration camp myself, but I spent two days and two nights between the German and Soviet cordons on a narrow strip of land no more than a third of a mile across when, toward the end of November 1939, I went illegally from one occupation to another on the lands of Poland. The Germans were letting everyone through in both directions, although they beat the Jews and robbed them of everything; the Soviets let no one through in either direction. On that patch of earth were camped nearly four thousand refugees—men, women, and children. During the day the first snow fell; by night we had a biting frost. The first night a loaf of bread cost a gold ring, the following day—two. On the second night on that no-man's-land, which was a great

THIS WAY FOR THE GAS, LADIES AND GENTLEMEN

field of stubble without a single tree or bush, sheds made out of boards sprang up. In them were sold hot soup and piroshki with kasha for gold and dollars. In the last shed, at the very end of the stubble, they were selling women.

"All of us walk around naked." The first story in this volume begins with an image that may seem similar to Dante's Inferno. "Twenty-eight thousand women have been stripped naked and driven out of the barracks. Now they swarm around the large yard between the block-houses. The heat rises, the hours are endless." They are naked as worms. Only later, when the scene draws nearer, as in a camera close-up, is it possible to distinguish in that wriggling mass of vermin different specimens of the same species: a few in pressed uniforms, with riding whips and high boots like glittering scales, and the common variety, with abdomens in stripes of blue and yellow. They differ also in weight: A few are well-nourished, fat, and sleek; the common types move their shriveled extremities with difficulty. Only their jaws are in constant motion. "Around us sit the Greeks, their jaws working greedily, like huge human insects. They munch on stale lumps of bread."

Borowski describes Auschwitz like an entomologist. The image of ants recurs many times, with their incessant march, day and night, night and day, from the ramp to the crematorium and from the barracks to the baths. The most terrifying thing in Borowski's stories is the icy detachment of the author. "You can get accustomed to the camp," says Vorarbeiter Tadeusz. Auschwitz is presented from a natural perspective—a day like any other. Everything is commonplace, routine, *normal*. ". . . first just one ordinary barn, brightly whitewashed—and here they proceed to asphyxiate people. Later, four large buildings, accommodating twenty thousand at a time without any trouble. No hocus-pocus, no poison, no hypnosis. Only several men directing traffic to keep operations running smoothly, and the thousands flow along like water from an open tap."

Auschwitz—with its black smoke from the crematoriums and its ditches clogged with corpses, there being no room for them in the ovens—is nothing out of the ordinary. "The camps, aren't they for people?" Auschwitz—with its whorehouse and its museum containing exhibits made of human skin, with its sports field where soccer is played and its concert hall where Beethoven is played— is merely an inevitable part of the world of stone. "Between two throw-ins in a soccer game, right behind my back, three thousand people had been put to death." Albert Camus wrote of the "logic of crime" and of the "crime of logic." For Borowski, the son of Soviet prisoners and the posthumous child of Auschwitz, the whole world is a concentration camp—was and will be. "What will the world know of us if the Germans win?"

Borowski called his book about Auschwitz "a voyage to the limit of a particular experience." At the limit of that experience Auschwitz is no exception but the rule. History is a sequence of Auschwitzes, one following the other. On his typhus-ridden straw mattress in the Auschwitz hospital he wrote, in a letter to his bald fiancée in the women's barracks: "You know how much I used to like Plato. Today I realize he lied. For the things of this world are not a reflection of the ideal, but a product of human sweat, blood and hard labor. It is we who built the pyramids, hewed the marble for the temples and the rocks for the imperial roads. . . . We were filthy and died real deaths. . . . What does ancient history say about us? . . . We rave over the extermination of the Etruscans, the destruction of Carthage, over treason, deceit, plunder. Roman law! Yes, today too there is a law!"

The Polish biographer entitled his book on Borowski *Escape from the World of Stone*. Borowski did not escape the world of stone. "The living," he wrote, "are always right, the dead are always wrong"—an optimistic statement. If the dead are wrong and the living are always right, everything is finally justified; but the story of Borowski's life and that which he wrote about Auschwitz show that the dead are right, and not the living.

JAN KOTT

This Way for the Gas, Ladies and Gentlemen

AND OTHER STORIES

This Way for the Gas,
Ladies and Gentlemen

All of us walk around naked. The delousing is finally over, and our striped suits are back from the tanks of Cyclone B solution, an efficient killer of lice in clothing and of men in gas chambers. Only the inmates in the blocks cut off from ours by the 'Spanish goats'* still have nothing to wear. But all the same, all of us walk around naked: the heat is unbearable. The camp has been sealed off tight. Not a single prisoner, not one solitary louse, can sneak through the gate. The labour Kommandos have stopped working. All day, thousands of naked men shuffle up and down the roads, cluster around the squares, or lie against the walls and on top of the roofs. We have been sleeping on plain boards, since our mattresses and blankets are still being disinfected. From the rear blockhouses we have a view of the F.K.L.—*Frauen Konzentration Lager*; there too the delousing is in full swing. Twenty-eight thousand women have been stripped naked and driven out of the barracks.

* Crossed wooden beams wrapped in barbed wire.

Now they swarm around the large yard between the block-houses.

The heat rises, the hours are endless. We are without even our usual diversion: the wide roads leading to the crematoria are empty. For several days now, no new transports have come in. Part of 'Canada'* has been liquidated and detailed to a labour Kommando—one of the very toughest—at Harmenz. For there exists in the camp a special brand of justice based on envy: when the rich and mighty fall, their friends see to it that they fall to the very bottom. And Canada, our Canada, which smells not of maple forests but of French perfume, has amassed great fortunes in diamonds and currency from all over Europe.

Several of us sit on the top bunk, our legs dangling over the edge. We slice the neat loaves of crisp, crunchy bread. It is a bit coarse to the taste, the kind that stays fresh for days. Sent all the way from Warsaw—only a week ago my mother held this white loaf in her hands ... dear Lord, dear Lord ...

We unwrap the bacon, the onion, we open a can of evaporated milk. Henri, the fat Frenchman, dreams aloud of the French wine brought by the transports from Strasbourg, Paris, Marseille ... Sweat streams down his body.

'Listen, *mon ami*, next time we go up on the loading ramp, I'll bring you real champagne. You haven't tried it before, eh?'

'No. But you'll never be able to smuggle it through the gate, so stop teasing. Why not try and "organize" some shoes for me instead—you know, the perforated kind, with a double sole, and what about that shirt you promised me long ago?'

* 'Canada' designated wealth and well-being in the camp. More specifically, it referred to the members of the labour gang, or Kommando, who helped to unload the incoming transports of people destined for the gas chambers.

'*Patience, patience.* When the new transports come, I'll bring all you want. We'll be going on the ramp again!'

'And what if there aren't any more "cremo" transports?' I say spitefully. 'Can't you see how much easier life is becoming around here: no limit on packages, no more beatings? You even write letters home ... One hears all kind of talk, and, dammit, they'll run out of people!'

'Stop talking nonsense.' Henri's serious fat face moves rhythmically, his mouth is full of sardines. We have been friends for a long time, but I do not even know his last name. 'Stop talking nonsense,' he repeats, swallowing with effort. 'They can't run out of people, or we'll starve to death in this blasted camp. All of us live on what they bring.'

'All? We have our packages ... '

'Sure, you and your friend, and ten other friends of yours. Some of you Poles get packages. But what about us, and the Jews, and the Russkis? And what if we had no food, no "organization" from the transports, do you think you'd be eating those packages of yours in peace? We wouldn't let you!'

'You would, you'd starve to death like the Greeks. Around here, whoever has grub, has power.'

'Anyway, you have enough, we have enough, so why argue?'

Right, why argue? They have enough, I have enough, we eat together and we sleep on the same bunks. Henri slices the bread, he makes a tomato salad. It tastes good with the commissary mustard.

Below us, naked, sweat-drenched men crowd the narrow barracks aisles or lie packed in eights and tens in the lower bunks. Their nude, withered bodies stink of sweat and excrement; their cheeks are hollow. Directly beneath me, in the bottom bunk, lies a rabbi. He has covered his head with a piece of rag torn off a blanket and reads from a

THIS WAY FOR THE GAS, LADIES AND GENTLEMEN

Hebrew prayer book (there is no shortage of this type of literature at the camp), wailing loudly, monotonously.

'Can't somebody shut him up? He's been raving as if he'd caught God himself by the feet.'

'I don't feel like moving. Let him rave. They'll take him to the oven that much sooner.'

'Religion is the opium of the people,' Henri, who is a Communist and a *rentier*, says sententiously. 'If they didn't believe in God and eternal life, they'd have smashed the crematoria long ago.'

'Why haven't you done it then?'

The question is rhetorical; the Frenchman ignores it.

'Idiot,' he says simply, and stuffs a tomato in his mouth.

Just as we finish our snack, there is a sudden commotion at the door. The Muslims* scurry in fright to the safety of their bunks, a messenger runs into the Block Elder's shack. The Elder, his face solemn, steps out at once.

'Canada! *Antreten!* But fast! There's a transport coming!'

'Great God!' yells Henri, jumping off the bunk. He swallows the rest of his tomato, snatches his coat, screams '*Raus*' at the men below, and in a flash is at the door. We can hear a scramble in the other bunks. Canada is leaving for the ramp.

'Henri, the shoes!' I call after him.

'*Keine Angst!*' he shouts back, already outside.

I proceed to put away the food. I tie a piece of rope around the suitcase where the onions and the tomatoes from my father's garden in Warsaw mingle with Portuguese sardines, bacon from Lublin (that's from my brother), and authentic sweetmeats from Salonica. I tie it all up, pull on my trousers, and slide off the bunk.

* 'Muslim' was the camp name for a prisoner who had been destroyed physically and spiritually, and who had neither the strength nor the will to go on living – a man ripe for the gas chamber.

'*Platz!*' I yell, pushing my way through the Greeks. They step aside. At the door I bump into Henri.

'*Was ist los?*'

'Want to come with us on the ramp?'

'Sure, why not?'

'Come along then, grab your coat! We're short of a few men. I've already told the Kapo,' and he shoves me out of the barracks door.

We line up. Someone has marked down our numbers, someone up ahead yells, 'March, march,' and now we are running towards the gate, accompanied by the shouts of a multilingual throng that is already being pushed back to the barracks. Not everybody is lucky enough to be going on the ramp ... We have almost reached the gate. *Links, zwei, drei, vier! Mützen ab!* Erect, arms stretched stiffly along our hips, we march past the gate briskly, smartly, almost gracefully. A sleepy S.S. man with a large pad in his hand checks us off, waving us ahead in groups of five.

'*Hundert!*' he calls after we have all passed.

'*Stimmt!*' comes a hoarse answer from out front.

We march fast, almost at a run. There are guards all around, young men with automatics. We pass camp II B, then some deserted barracks and a clump of unfamiliar green—apple and pear trees. We cross the circle of watch-towers and, running, burst on to the highway. We have arrived. Just a few more yards. There, surrounded by trees, is the ramp.

A cheerful little station, very much like any other provincial railway stop: a small square framed by tall chestnuts and paved with yellow gravel. Not far off, beside the road, squats a tiny wooden shed, uglier and more flimsy then the ugliest and flimsiest railway shack; farther along lie stacks of old rails, heaps of wooden beams, barracks parts, bricks, paving stones. This is where they load freight for Birkenau: supplies for the construction

33

of the camp, and people for the gas chambers. Trucks drive around, load up lumber, cement, people—a regular daily routine.

And now the guards are being posted along the rails, across the beams, in the green shade of the Silesian chestnuts, to form a tight circle around the ramp. They wipe the sweat from their faces and sip out of their canteens. It is unbearably hot; the sun stands motionless at its zenith.

'Fall out!'

We sit down in the narrow streaks of shade along the stacked rails. The hungry Greeks (several of them managed to come along, God only knows how) rummage underneath the rails. One of them finds some pieces of mildewed bread, another a few half-rotten sardines. They eat.

'*Schweinedreck*,' spits a young, tall guard with corn-coloured hair and dreamy blue eyes. 'For God's sake, any minute you'll have so much food to stuff down your guts, you'll bust!' He adjusts his gun, wipes his face with a handkerchief.

'Hey you, fatso!' His boot lightly touches Henri's shoulder. '*Pass mal auf*, want a drink?'

'Sure, but I haven't got any marks,' replies the Frenchman with a professional air.

'*Schade*, too bad.'

'Come, come, Herr Posten, isn't my word good enough any more? Haven't we done business before? How much?'

'One hundred. *Gemacht?*'

'*Gemacht.*'

We drink the water, lukewarm and tasteless. It will be paid for by the people who have not yet arrived.

'Now you be careful,' says Henri, turning to me. He tosses away the empty bottle. It strikes the rails and bursts into tiny fragments. 'Don't take any money, they might be checking. Anyway, who the hell needs money? You've got enough to eat. Don't take suits, either, or they'll think

34

you're planning to escape. Just get a shirt, silk only, with a collar. And a vest. And if you find something to drink, don't bother calling me. I know how to shift for myself, but you watch your step or they'll let you have it.'

'Do they beat you up here?'

'Naturally. You've got to have eyes in your ass. *Arsch-augen*.'

Around us sit the Greeks, their jaws working greedily, like huge human insects. They munch on stale lumps of bread. They are restless, wondering what will happen next. The sight of the large beams and the stacks of rails has them worried. They dislike carrying heavy loads.

'*Was wir arbeiten?*' they ask.

'*Niks. Transport kommen, alles Krematorium, compris?*'

'*Alles verstehen,*' they answer in crematorium Esperanto. All is well—they will not have to move the heavy rails or carry the beams.

In the meantime, the ramp has become increasingly alive with activity, increasingly noisy. The crews are being divided into those who will open and unload the arriving cattle cars and those who will be posted by the wooden steps. They receive instructions on how to proceed most efficiently. Motor cycles drive up, delivering S.S. officers, bemedalled, glittering with brass, beefy men with highly polished boots and shiny, brutal faces. Some have brought their briefcases, others hold thin, flexible whips. This gives them an air of military readiness and agility. They walk in and out of the commissary—for the miserable little shack by the road serves as their commissary, where in the summer-time they drink mineral water, *Studentenquelle*, and where in winter they can warm up with a glass of hot wine. They greet each other in the state-approved way, raising an arm Roman fashion, then shake hands cordially, ex-change warm smiles, discuss mail from home, their child-ren, their families. Some stroll majestically on the ramp.

The silver squares on their collars glitter, the gravel crunches under their boots, their bamboo whips snap impatiently.

We lie against the rails in the narrow streaks of shade, breathe unevenly, occasionally exchange a few words in our various tongues, and gaze listlessly at the majestic men in green uniforms, at the green trees, and at the church steeple of a distant village.

'The transport is coming,' somebody says. We spring to our feet, all eyes turn in one direction. Around the bend, one after another, the cattle cars begin rolling in. The train backs into the station, a conductor leans out, waves his hand, blows a whistle. The locomotive whistles back with a shrieking noise, puffs, the train rolls slowly alongside the ramp. In the tiny barred windows appear pale, wilted, exhausted human faces, terror-stricken women with tangled hair, unshaven men. They gaze at the station in silence. And then, suddenly, there is a stir inside the cars and a pounding against the wooden boards.

'Water! Air!'—weary, desperate cries.

Heads push through the windows, mouths gasp frantically for air. They draw a few breaths, then disappear; others come in their place, then also disappear. The cries and moans grow louder.

A man in a green uniform covered with more glitter than any of the others jerks his head impatiently, his lips twist in annoyance. He inhales deeply, then with a rapid gesture throws his cigarette away and signals to the guard. The guard removes the automatic from his shoulder, aims, sends a series of shots along the train. All is quiet now. Meanwhile, the trucks have arrived, steps are being drawn up, and the Canada men stand ready at their posts by the train doors. The S.S. officer with the briefcase raises his hand.

'Whoever takes gold, or anything at all besides food,

will be shot for stealing Reich property. Understand? *Verstanden?*'

'*Jawohl!*' we answer eagerly.

'*Also los!* Begin!'

The bolts crack, the doors fall open. A wave of fresh air rushes inside the train. People ... inhumanly crammed, buried under incredible heaps of luggage, suitcases, trunks, packages, crates, bundles of every description (everything that had been their past and was to start their future). Monstrously squeezed together, they have fainted from heat, suffocated, crushed one another. Now they push towards the opened doors, breathing like fish cast out on the sand.

'Attention! Out, and take your luggage with you! Take out everything. Pile all your stuff near the exits. Yes, your coats too. It is summer. March to the left. Understand?'

'Sir, what's going to happen to us?' They jump from the train on to the gravel, anxious, worn-out.

'Where are you people from?'

'Sosnowiec-Będzin. Sir, what's going to happen to us?' They repeat the question stubbornly, gazing into our tired eyes.

'I don't know, I don't understand Polish.'

It is the camp law: people going to their death must be deceived to the very end. This is the only permissible form of charity. The heat is tremendous. The sun hangs directly over our heads, the white, hot sky quivers, the air vibrates, an occasional breeze feels like a sizzling blast from a furnace. Our lips are parched, the mouth fills with the salty taste of blood, the body is weak and heavy from lying in the sun. Water!

A huge, multicoloured wave of people loaded down with luggage pours from the train like a blind, mad river trying to find a new bed. But before they have a chance to recover, before they can draw a breath of fresh air and look at the sky, bundles are snatched from their hands, coats ripped off their backs, their purses and umbrellas taken away.

'But please, sir, it's for the sun, I cannot ... '

'*Verboten!*' one of us barks through clenched teeth. There is an S.S. man standing behind your back, calm, efficient, watchful.

'*Meine Herrschaften*, this way, ladies and gentlemen, try not to throw your things around, please. Show some goodwill,' he says courteously, his restless hands playing with the slender whip.

'Of course, of course,' they answer as they pass, and now they walk alongside the train somewhat more cheerfully. A woman reaches down quickly to pick up her handbag. The whip flies, the woman screams, stumbles, and falls under the feet of the surging crowd. Behind her, a child cries in a thin little voice 'Mamele!'—a very small girl with tangled black curls.

The heaps grow. Suitcases, bundles, blankets, coats, handbags that open as they fall, spilling coins, gold, watches; mountains of bread pile up at the exits, heaps of marmalade, jams, masses of meat, sausages; sugar spills on the gravel. Trucks, loaded with people, start up with a deafening roar and drive off amidst the wailing and screaming of the women separated from their children, and the stupefied silence of the men left behind. They are the ones who had been ordered to step to the right—the healthy and the young who will go to the camp. In the end, they too will not escape death, but first they must work.

Trucks leave and return, without interruption, as on a monstrous conveyor belt. A Red Cross van drives back and forth, back and forth, incessantly: it transports the gas that will kill these people. The enormous cross on the hood, red as blood, seems to dissolve in the sun.

The Canada men at the trucks cannot stop for a single moment, even to catch their breath. They shove the people up the steps, pack them in tightly, sixty per truck, more or less. Near by stands a young, cleanshaven 'gentleman', an S.S. officer with a notebook in his hand. For each departing truck he enters a mark; sixteen gone means one thousand people, more or less. The gentleman is calm, precise. No truck can leave without a signal from him, or a mark in his notebook: *Ordnung muss sein*. The marks swell into thousands, the thousands into whole transports, which afterwards we shall simply call 'from Salonica', 'from Strasbourg', 'from Rotterdam'. This one will be called 'Sosnowiec-Będzin'. The new prisoners from Sosnowiec-Będzin will receive serial numbers 131-2—thousand, of course, though afterwards we shall simply say 131-2, for short.

The transports swell into weeks, months, years. When the war is over, they will count up the marks in their notebooks—all four and a half million of them. The bloodiest battle of the war, the greatest victory of the strong, united Germany. *Ein Reich, ein Volk, ein Führer*—and four crematoria.

The train has been emptied. A thin, pock-marked S.S. man peers inside, shakes his head in disgust and motions to our group, pointing his finger at the door.

'*Rein*. Clean it up!'

We climb inside. In the corners amid human excrement and abandoned wrist-watches lie squashed, trampled infants, naked little monsters with enormous heads and bloated bellies. We carry them out like chickens, holding several in each hand.

'Don't take them to the trucks, pass them on to the women,' says the S.S. man, lighting a cigarette. His cigarette lighter is not working properly; he examines it carefully.

39

'Take them, for God's sake!' I explode as the women run from me in horror, covering their eyes.

The name of God sounds strangely pointless, since the women and the infants will go on the trucks, every one of them, without exception. We all know what this means, and we look at each other with hate and horror.

'What, you don't want to take them?' asks the pock-marked S.S. man with a note of surprise and reproach in his voice, and reaches for his revolver.

'You mustn't shoot, I'll carry them.' A tall, grey-haired woman takes the little corpses out of my hands and for an instant gazes straight into my eyes.

'My poor boy,' she whispers and smiles at me. Then she walks away, staggering along the path. I lean against the side of the train. I am terribly tired. Someone pulls at my sleeve.

'*En avant*, to the rails, come on!'

I look up, but the face swims before my eyes, dissolves, huge and transparent, melts into the motionless trees and the sea of people ... I blink rapidly: Henri.

'Listen, Henri, are we good people?'

'That's stupid. Why do you ask?'

'You see, my friend, you see, I don't know why, but I am furious, simply furious with these people—furious because I must be here because of them. I feel no pity. I am not sorry they're going to the gas chamber. Damn them all! I could throw myself at them, beat them with my fists. It must be pathological, I just can't understand ... '

'Ah, on the contrary, it is natural, predictable, calcu-lated. The ramp exhausts you, you rebel—and the easiest way to relieve your hate is to turn against someone weaker. Why, I'd even call it healthy. It's simple logic, *compris*?' He props himself up comfortably against the heap of rails. 'Look at the Greeks, they know how to make the best of it! They stuff their bellies with anything they find. One of them has just devoured a full jar of marmalade.'

'Pigs! Tomorrow half of them will die of the shits.'

'Pigs? You've been hungry.'

'Pigs!' I repeat furiously. I close my eyes. The air is filled with ghastly cries, the earth trembles beneath me, I can feel sticky moisture on my eyelids. My throat is completely dry.

The morbid procession streams on and on—trucks growl like mad dogs. I shut my eyes tight, but I can still see corpses dragged from the train, trampled infants, cripples piled on top of the dead, wave after wave ... freight cars roll in, the heaps of clothing, suitcases and bundles grow, people climb out, look at the sun, take a few breaths, beg for water, get into the trucks, drive away. And again freight cars roll in, again people ... The scenes become confused in my mind—I am not sure if all of this is actually happening, or if I am dreaming. There is a humming inside my head; I feel that I must vomit.

Henri tugs at my arm.

'Don't sleep, we're off to load up the loot.'

All the people are gone. In the distance, the last few trucks roll along the road in clouds of dust, the train has left, several S.S. officers promenade up and down the ramp. The silver glitters on their collars. Their boots shine, their red, beefy faces shine. Among them there is a woman—only now I realize she has been here all along—withered, flat-chested, bony, her thin, colourless hair pulled back and tied in a 'Nordic' knot; her hands are in the pockets of her wide skirt. With a rat-like, resolute smile glued on her thin lips she sniffs around the corners of the ramp. She detests feminine beauty with the hatred of a woman who is herself repulsive, and knows it. Yes, I have seen her many times before and I know her well: she is the commandant of the F.K.L. She has come to look over

41

the new crop of women, for some of them, instead of going on the trucks, will go on foot—to the concentration camp. There our boys, the barbers from Zauna, will shave their heads and will have a good laugh at their 'outside world' modesty.

We proceed to load the loot. We lift huge trunks, heave them on to the trucks. There they are arranged in stacks, packed tightly. Occasionally somebody slashes one open with a knife, for pleasure or in search of vodka and perfume. One of the crates falls open; suits, shirts, books drop out on the ground ... I pick up a small, heavy package. I unwrap it—gold, about two handfuls, bracelets, rings, brooches, diamonds ...

'Gib hier,' an S.S. man says calmly, holding up his briefcase already full of gold and colourful foreign currency. He locks the case, hands it to an officer, takes another, an empty one, and stands by the next truck, waiting. The gold will go to the Reich.

It is hot, terribly hot. Our throats are dry, each word hurts. Anything for a sip of water! Faster, faster, so that it is over, so that we may rest. At last we are done, all the trucks have gone. Now we swiftly clean up the remaining dirt: there must be 'no trace left of the Schweinerei'. But just as the last truck disappears behind the trees and we walk, finally, to rest in the shade, a shrill whistle sounds around the bend. Slowly, terribly slowly, a train rolls in, the engine whistles back with a deafening shriek. Again weary, pale faces at the windows, flat as though cut out of paper, with huge, feverishly burning eyes. Already trucks are pulling up, already the composed gentleman with the notebook is at his post, and the S.S. men emerge from the commissary carrying briefcases for the gold and money. We unseal the train doors.

It is impossible to control oneself any longer. Brutally we tear suitcases from their hands, impatiently pull off their coats. Go on, go on, vanish! They go, they vanish. Men, women, children. Some of them know.

Here is a woman—she walks quickly, but tries to appear calm. A small child with a pink cherub's face runs after her and, unable to keep up, stretches out his little arms and cries: 'Mama! Mama!'

'Pick up your child, woman!'

'It's not mine, sir, not mine!' she shouts hysterically and runs on, covering her face with her hands. She wants to hide, she wants to reach those who will not ride the trucks, those who will go on foot, those who will stay alive. She is young, healthy, good-looking, she wants to live.

But the child runs after her, wailing loudly: 'Mama, mama, don't leave me!'

'It's not mine, not mine, no!'

Andrei, a sailor from Sevastopol, grabs hold of her. His eyes are glassy from vodka and the heat. With one powerful blow he knocks her off her feet, then, as she falls, takes her by the hair and pulls her up again. His face twitches with rage.

'Ah, you bloody Jewess! So you're running from your own child! I'll show you, you whore!' His huge hand chokes her, he lifts her in the air and heaves her on to the truck like a heavy sack of grain.

'Here! And take this with you, bitch!' and he throws the child at her feet.

'*Gut gemacht*, good work. That's the way to deal with degenerate mothers,' says the S.S. man standing at the foot of the truck. '*Gut, gut, Russki*.'

'Shut your mouth,' growls Andrei through clenched teeth, and walks away. From under a pile of rags he pulls out a canteen, unscrews the cork, takes a few deep swallows, passes it to me. The strong vodka burns the throat. My head swims, my legs are shaky, again I feel like throwing up.

And suddenly, above the teeming crowd pushing forward like a river driven by an unseen power, a girl appears. She descends lightly from the train, hops on to the gravel, looks around inquiringly, as if somewhat surprised. Her soft, blonde hair has fallen on her shoulders in a torrent, she throws it back impatiently. With a natural gesture she runs her hands down her blouse, casually straightens her skirt. She stands like this for an instant, gazing at the crowd, then turns and with a gliding look examines our faces, as though searching for someone. Unknowingly, I continue to stare at her, until our eyes meet.

'Listen, tell me, where are they taking us?'

I look at her without saying a word. Here, standing before me, is a girl, a girl with enchanting blonde hair, with beautiful breasts, wearing a little cotton blouse, a girl with a wise, mature look in her eyes. Here she stands, gazing straight into my face, waiting. And over there is the gas chamber: communal death, disgusting and ugly. And over in the other direction is the concentration camp: the shaved head, the heavy Soviet trousers in sweltering heat, the sickening, stale odour of dirty, damp female bodies, the animal hunger, the inhuman labour, and later the same gas chamber, only an even more hideous, more terrible death …

Why did she bring it? I think to myself, noticing a lovely gold watch on her delicate wrist. They'll take it away from her anyway.

'Listen, tell me,' she repeats.

I remain silent. Her lips tighten.

'I know,' she says with a shade of proud contempt in her voice, tossing her head. She walks off resolutely in the direction of the trucks. Someone tries to stop her; she boldly pushes him aside and runs up the steps. In the distance I can only catch a glimpse of her blonde hair flying in the breeze.

44

I go back inside the train; I carry out dead infants; I unload luggage. I touch corpses, but I cannot overcome the mounting, uncontrollable terror. I try to escape from the corpses, but they are everywhere: lined up on the gravel, on the cement edge of the ramp, inside the cattle cars. Babies, hideous naked women, men twisted by convulsions. I run off as far as I can go, but immediately a whip slashes across my back. Out of the corner of my eye I see an S.S. man, swearing profusely. I stagger forward and run, lose myself in the Canada group. Now, at last, I can once more rest against the stack of rails. The sun has leaned low over the horizon and illuminates the ramp with a reddish glow; the shadows of the trees have become elongated, ghostlike. In the silence that settles over nature at this time of day, the human cries seem to rise all the way to the sky.

Only from this distance does one have a full view of the inferno on the teeming ramp. I see a pair of human beings who have fallen to the ground locked in a last desperate embrace. The man has dug his fingers into the woman's flesh and has caught her clothing with his teeth. She screams hysterically, swears, cries, until at last a large boot comes down over her throat and she is silent. They are pulled apart and dragged like cattle to the truck. I see four Canada men lugging a corpse: a huge, swollen female corpse. Cursing, dripping wet from the strain, they kick out of their way some stray children who have been running all over the ramp, howling like dogs. The men pick them up by the collars, heads, arms, and toss them inside the trucks, on top of the heaps. The four men have trouble lifting the fat corpse on to the car, they call others for help, and all together they hoist up the mound of meat. Big, swollen, puffed-up corpses are being collected from all over the ramp; on top of them are piled the invalids, the smothered, the sick, the unconscious. The heap seethes, howls, groans. The driver starts the motor, the truck begins rolling.

'Halt! Halt!' an S.S. man yells after them. 'Stop, damn you!'

They are dragging to the truck an old man wearing tails and a band around his arm. His head knocks against the gravel and pavement; he moans and wails in an uninterrupted monotone: *'Ich will mit dem Herrn Kommandanten sprechen*—I wish to speak with the commandant ... ' With senile stubbornness he keeps repeating these words all the way. Thrown on the truck, trampled by others, choked, he still wails: *'Ich will mit dem ...'*

'Look here, old man!' a young S.S. man calls, laughing jovially. 'In half an hour you'll be talking with the top commandant! Only don't forget to greet him with a *Heil Hitler!'*

Several other men are carrying a small girl with only one leg. They hold her by the arms and the one leg. Tears are running down her face and she whispers faintly: 'Sir, it hurts, it hurts ... ' They throw her on the truck on top of the corpses. She will burn alive along with them.

The evening has come, cool and clear. The stars are out. We lie against the rails. It is incredibly quiet. Anaemic bulbs hang from the top of the high lamp-posts; beyond the circle of light stretches an impenetrable darkness. Just one step, and a man could vanish for ever. But the guards are watching, their automatics ready.

'Did you get the shoes?' asks Henri.

'No.'

'Why?'

'My God, man, I am finished, absolutely finished!'

'So soon? After only two transports? Just look at me, I ... since Christmas, at least a million people have passed through my hands. The worst of all are the transports from around Paris—one is always bumping into friends.'

'And what do you say to them?'

'That first they will have a bath, and later we'll meet at the camp. What would you say?'

I do not answer. We drink coffee with vodka; somebody opens a tin of cocoa and mixes it with sugar. We scoop it up by the handful, the cocoa sticks to the lips. Again coffee, again vodka.

'Henri, what are we waiting for?'

'There'll be another transport.'

'I'm not going to unload it! I can't take any more.'

'So, it's got you down? Canada is nice, eh?' Henri grins indulgently and disappears into the darkness. In a moment he is back again.

'All right. Just sit here quietly and don't let an S.S. man see you. I'll try to find you your shoes.'

'Just leave me alone. Never mind the shoes.' I want to sleep. It is very late.

Another whistle, another transport. Freight cars emerge out of the darkness, pass under the lamp-posts, and again vanish in the night. The ramp is small, but the circle of lights is smaller. The unloading will have to be done gradually. Somewhere the trucks are growling. They back up against the steps, black, ghostlike, their searchlights flash across the trees. *Wasser! Luft!* The same all over again, like a late showing of the same film: a volley of shots, the train falls silent. Only this time a little girl pushes herself halfway through the small window and, losing her balance, falls out on to the gravel. Stunned, she lies still for a moment, then stands up and begins walking around in a circle, faster and faster, waving her rigid arms in the air, breathing loudly and spasmodically, whining in a faint voice. Her mind has given way in the inferno inside the train. The whining is hard on the nerves: an S.S. man approaches calmly, his heavy boot strikes between her shoulders. She falls. Holding her down with his foot, he draws his revolver, fires once, then again. She remains face down, kicking the gravel with her feet, until she stiffens. They proceed to unseal the train.

I am back on the ramp, standing by the doors. A warm, sickening smell gushes from inside. The mountain of people filling the car almost halfway up to the ceiling is motionless, horribly tangled, but still steaming.

'*Ausladen!*' comes the command. An S.S. man steps out from the darkness. Across his chest hangs a portable searchlight. He throws a stream of light inside.

'Why are you standing about like sheep? Start unloading!' His whip flies and falls across our backs. I seize a corpse by the hand; the fingers close tightly around mine. I pull back with a shriek and stagger away. My heart pounds, jumps up to my throat. I can no longer control the nausea. Hunched under the train I begin to vomit. Then, like a drunk, I weave over to the stack of rails.

I lie against the cool, kind metal and dream about returning to the camp, about my bunk, on which there is no mattress, about sleep among comrades who are not going to the gas tonight. Suddenly I see the camp as a haven of peace. It is true, others may be dying, but one is somehow still alive, one has enough food, enough strength to work ...

The lights on the ramp flicker with a spectral glow, the wave of people—feverish, agitated, stupefied people—flows on and on, endlessly. They think that now they will have to face a new life in the camp, and they prepare themselves emotionally for the hard struggle ahead. They do not know that in just a few moments they will die, that the gold, money, and diamonds which they have so prudently hidden in their clothing and on their bodies are now useless to them. Experienced professionals will probe into every recess of their flesh, will pull the gold from under the tongue and the diamonds from the uterus and the colon. They will rip out gold teeth. In tightly sealed crates they will ship them to Berlin.

The S.S. men's black figures move about, dignified, businesslike. The gentleman with the notebook puts down his final marks, rounds out the figures: fifteen thousand.

Many, very many, trucks have been driven to the crematoria today.

It is almost over. The dead are being cleared off the ramp and piled into the last truck. The Canada men, weighed down under a load of bread, marmalade and sugar, and smelling of perfume and fresh linen, line up to go. For several days the entire camp will live off this transport. For several days the entire camp will talk about 'Sosnowiec-Będzin'. 'Sosnowiec-Będzin' was a good, rich transport.

The stars are already beginning to pale as we walk back to the camp. The sky grows translucent and opens high above our heads—it is getting light.

Great columns of smoke rise from the crematoria and merge up above into a huge black river which very slowly floats across the sky over Birkenau and disappears beyond the forests in the direction of Trzebinia. The 'Sosnowiec-Będzin' transport is already burning.

We pass a heavily armed S.S. detachment on its way to change guard. The men march briskly, in step, shoulder to shoulder, one mass, one will.

'*Und morgen die ganze Welt* ... ' they sing at the top of their lungs.

'*Rechts ran!* To the right march!' snaps a command from up front. We move out of their way.

A Day at
Harmenz

I

The shadows of the chestnut trees are green and soft.
They sway gently over the ground, still moist after being
newly turned over, and rise up in sea-green cupolas scented
with the morning freshness. The trees form a high palisade
along the road, their crowns dissolve into the hue of
the sky. From the direction of the ponds comes the heavy,
intoxicating smell of the marshes. The grass, green and
velvety, is still silvered with dew, but the earth already
steams in the sun. It will be a hot day.

But the shade under the chestnut trees is green and soft.
I sit in the sand beneath its cover, and with a large adjust-
able wrench tighten up the fishplates along the railway
tracks. The wrench is cool and fits comfortably in my
hand. I strike it against the rails at even intervals. A firm
metallic sound reverberates throughout all Harmenz and
comes back from afar in an unfamiliar echo. Several Greeks
have gathered around me. They stand resting on their
spades. But the men from Salonica and the vineyards of

Macedonia do not like the shade. They stand in the open, remove their shirts, and expose to the sun their unbelievably thin shoulders covered with scabs and sores. It is getting hot.

'Working hard today, aren't you? Good morning, Tadek. How would you like something to eat?'

'Good morning, Mrs Haneczka! No thanks. Actually, I am just banging so hard because of our new Kapo ... Forgive me for not getting up, but, you understand: there's a war on, *Bewegung, Arbeit* ... '

Mrs Haneczka smiles.

'Of course I understand. You know, I wouldn't have recognized you if I hadn't known it was you. Do you remember when you used to hide in the bushes to eat the unpeeled potatoes I stole for you from the chicken house?'

'Eat them? My dear lady, I devoured them! Careful, here comes the S.S.'

Mrs Haneczka threw a handful of grain from her sieve to the chickens that came running from all directions. Then, as she looked around, she shrugged.

'Oh, it's only the chief. I can twist him around my little finger.'

'Around such a tiny finger? You are a very brave woman.'

I slammed the wrench hard against the rails, trying to beat out 'La donna è mobile' in her honour.

'For heaven's sake, don't make so much noise! But seriously, how about something to eat? I'm on my way to the house, I could bring you something.'

'Thank you most kindly, Mrs Haneczka, but I think you fed me quite enough when I was poor ... '

' ... poor, but honest,' she finished with a touch of irony.

'Well, helpless, at any rate,' I retorted. 'But speaking of helplessness, I had two fine pieces of soap for you, called by the most beautiful of all names, "Warsaw", and ... '

' ... and, someone's stolen them, as usual?'

'Someone's stolen them, as usual. When I had nothing, I slept in peace. And now! No matter how well I wrap my packages and tie them with string and wire, someone always manages to get them. A few days ago they "organized" a jar of honey off me, and now the soap. But just wait till I catch the thief!'

Mrs Haneczka laughed.

'I can imagine ... Don't be such a child! As for the soap, you really needn't worry. I got two cakes today, from Ivan. Oh, I almost forgot, please give Ivan this little packet, it's a piece of lard,' and she laid a small package at the foot of the tree. 'See, here's the soap he gave me.'

She unwrapped it; it looked strangely familiar. I went over and examined it more closely. On both of the large cakes was imprinted the cameo of King Sigismund and the word 'Warsaw'.

I handed the package back to her without a word.

'Yes, very fine soap,' I said after a moment.

I looked across the field, towards the scattered groups of workers. In one group, right by the potatoes, I spotted Ivan. He was circling watchfully around his men like a sheepdog, calling out words I could not make out at that distance, and waving his tall wooden stick.

'Just wait till I catch the thief,' I repeated, not realizing that I was talking to empty space. Mrs Haneczka had left. From the distance, she turned and called back:

'Dinner as usual, under the chestnuts!'

'Thank you!'

Again I began to strike the wrench against the rails and tighten up the loose bolts.

Mrs Haneczka was popular with the Greeks, since from time to time she brought them a few potatoes.

'Mrs Haneczka *gut, extra prima*. Is she your Madonna?'

'My Madonna?' I protested, inadvertently striking my finger with the wrench. 'She's a friend, see? *Camarade, filos, compris Greco bandito?*'

'*Greco niks bandito, Greco gut man.* But why you not eat from her? *Patatas?*'

'I'm not hungry. I have enough to eat.'

'*Nix gut, nix gut.*' The old porter from Salonica who knew twelve Southern languages shook his head. 'We are hungry, always hungry, always, always ... '

He stretched out his bony arms. Under the skin covered with scabs and sores, the muscles played with a strangely distinct movement, as though they were quite separate from the rest of him. A smile softened the outline of his tense face, but could not extinguish the permanent fever in his eyes.

'If you're hungry, ask her for food yourself. Let her give it to you. And now go on back to work, *laborando, laborando*, I'm getting tired of you.'

'No, Tadek, I think you are wrong,' spoke up an old, fat Jew, stepping out from behind. He rested his spade on the ground and, standing over me, continued: 'You've been hungry too, so you should be able to understand us. What would it cost you to ask her for a bucket of potatoes?'

He drawled out the word 'bucket' with relish.

'Get off my back, Becker—you and your philosophy—and stick to your digging, *compris*? And let me tell you something: when your time comes to go to the gas, I'll help you along personally, and with great pleasure. D'you want to know why?'

'Why, in God's name?'

'Because of Poznań. Or isn't it true that you were a camp senior at the Jewish camp outside Poznań?'

'Well, what if it is?'

'And isn't it true that you killed your own people? And

53

that you hanged them on the post* for every bit of stolen margarine or bread?'

'I hanged thieves.'

'Listen, Becker, they say your son is in quarantine.'

Becker's fingers tightened around the spade handle; his eyes began to appraise my body, my neck, my head.

'You better let go of that spade, and stop looking at me with such murderous eyes. Tell me, is it true that your own son has given orders to have you killed, because of Poznań?'

'It is true,' he said darkly. 'And it is also true that in Poznań I personally hanged my other son, and not by the arms, but by the neck. He stole bread.'

'You swine!' I exploded.

But Becker, the old, melancholy, silver-haired Jew, had already calmed down. He looked down at me almost with pity and asked:

'How long have you been in the camp?'

'Oh, a few months.'

'You know something, Tadek, I think you're a nice boy,' he said unexpectedly, 'but you haven't really known hunger, have you?'

'That depends on what you mean by hunger.'

'Real hunger is when one man regards another man as something to eat. I have been hungry like that, you see.' Since I said nothing but only banged the wrench against the rails from time to time, mechanically looking left and right to see if the Kapo was around, he continued: 'Our camp, over there, was small ... Right next to a road. Many people walked along that road, well-dressed men, women too. They passed on their way to church on Sundays, for instance. Or there were couples out for a stroll. And a little

* Hanging a man on a post was a form of punishment reserved for minor infractions. It consisted of tying a man's hands behind his back and placing him on a post until his arms came out of their sockets.

farther on was a village, just an ordinary village. There, people had everything, only half a mile from us. And we had turnips ... good God, our people were ready to eat each other! So, you see, wasn't I to kill the cooks who bought vodka with our butter, and cigarettes with our bread? My son stole, so I killed him, too. I am a porter, I know life.'

I looked at him with curiosity, as though I had never seen him before.

'And you, you never ate anything but your own ration?'

'That was different. I was a camp senior.'

'Look out! *Laborando, laborando, presto!*' I yelled suddenly, for from around a bend in the road came an S.S. man on a bicycle. As he rode by, he eyed us closely. All backs bent down, all spades were lifted heavily in the air. I began to hammer furiously against the rails.

The S.S. man vanished beyond the trees. The spades stopped moving; the Greeks lapsed into their usual torpor.

'What time is it?'

'I don't know. It's a long time yet till dinner. But you know, Becker? I'll tell you this in parting: today there's going to be a selection in the camp. I sincerely hope that you, along with your scabs and sores, go straight to the chimney!'

'A selection? How do you know ... '

'Upset you, didn't I? There's going to be one, that's all. Scared, eh? You know the story about the wolf ... ' I smiled spitefully at my own wit and walked away humming a popular camp tango called 'Cremo'. The Jew's empty eyes, suddenly void of all content, stared fixedly into space.

II

The railway tracks on which I was working criss-crossed the whole field. At one end I had taken them right up to

55

a heap of burned bones which a truck had brought from the crematoria; the other end I had run to the pond, where the bones were to be finally deposited; in one spot I took them up to a mound of sand, which was to be spread level over the field to give a dry base to the marshy soil; elsewhere I laid them along an embankment used for collecting sand. The tracks ran this way and that, and wherever they intersected there was an enormous turntable, which had to be shifted from one spot to another.

A group of half-naked men surrounded the turntable, bent down and clutched it with their fingers.

'*Hooch!* Up!' I screamed, raising my hand like an orchestra conductor for better effect. The men tugged, once, and again. One of them fell heavily over the turntable, unable to stay on his feet. Kicked repeatedly by his comrades, he crawled out of the ring and, lifting his face smeared with sand and tears off the ground, groaned:

'*Zu schwer, zu schwer* ... It's too heavy, comrade, too heavy...' Then he thrust his bloody fist into his mouth and sucked greedily.

'Back to work, *auf!* Up with you! Now, once more! *Hooch!* Up!'

'Up!' repeated the men in an even chorus. They bent down as low as they could, arched their bony, fish-like backs, straining every muscle in their bodies. But the hands clinging to the turntable hung limp and helpless.

'Up!'

'Up!'

Suddenly a rain of blows fell across the ring of arched backs, bowed shoulders, and heads bent almost to the ground. A spade struck against skulls, slashed the skin through to the bone, slammed across bellies with a hollow groan. The men swarmed around the turntable. And all at once there was a terrible roar; the turntable moved, rose in the air and, swaying uncertainly above the men's heads, started forward, threatening to fall at any moment.

'You dogs!' shouted the Kapo after them. 'Can't you do anything without help from me?' Breathing heavily he rubbed his crimson, swollen face and ran an absent gaze over the group as if seeing them for the first time. Then he turned to me:

'You there, railway man! Hot today, isn't it?'

'It is, Kapo. That turntable should be put down by the third incubator, right? And what about the rails?'

'Run them right up to the ditch.'

'But there's an embankment in the way.'

'Then dig through it. The job must be finished by noon. And by evening make me four stretchers. Maybe some corpses will have to be carried back to camp. Hot today, eh?'

'Yes, but Kapo ...'

'Listen, railway man, let me have a lemon.'

'Send your boy over later. I haven't got one on me.'

He nodded a few times and walked away, limping. He was going to the house for some food, but I knew he would get nothing there, as long as he kept on beating the prisoners. We set the turntable down. With a terrible effort we pulled the rails up to it, levered them into position, tightened up the bolts with our bare hands. Finally the hungry, feverish men lay down to rest, their bodies weak, bloodstained. The sun hung high in the sky, the heat was growing deadly.

'What time is it, comrade?'

'Ten,' I answered without lifting my eyes from the rails.

'Lord, Lord, still two hours till dinner. Is it true that there's to be a selection in the camp today, that we'll all go to the cremo?'

They already knew about the selection. Secretly, they dressed their wounds, trying to make them cleaner and fewer; they tore off their bandages, massaged their muscles, splashed themselves with water so as to be fresher and more agile for the evening. They fought for their existence fiercely and heroically. But some no longer cared. They moved only to avoid being whipped, devoured grass and sticky clay to keep from feeling too much hunger; they walked around in a daze, like living corpses.

'All of us ... crematorium. But all Germans will be *kaput*. War *fini*, all Germans ... crematorium. All: women, children. Understand?'

'I understand, *Greco gut*. Don't worry, there won't be any selection, *keine Angst*.'

I dug across the embankment. The light, handy spade virtually worked by itself in my hands. The slabs of wet earth yielded easily and flew softly in the air. Work is not unpleasant when one has eaten a breakfast of smoked bacon with bread and garlic and washed it down with a tin of evaporated milk.

The Kommandoführer, a sickly little S.S. man, worn out from walking among the diggers, had seated himself in the meagre shade under the brick incubator, his shirt unbuttoned on his thin chest. He was an expert in lashing a whip. Only the day before I had felt it twice on my own back.

'What's new, plate layer?'

I swung my spade, slicing through the top layers of earth.

'Three hundred thousand Bolsheviks have fallen at Orzel.'

'That's good news, no? What do you think?'

'Sure it's good news. Especially since the same number of Germans were killed too. And the Bolsheviks will be up here before the year is out, if things continue this way.'

'You think so?' He smiled bitterly and repeated the ritual question: 'How much longer to dinner?'

I took out my watch, an old piece of junk with funny Roman numbers. I was fond of it because it reminded me of a watch my father used to own. I bought it at the camp for a packet of figs.

'It's eleven.'

The German got up from under the brick wall and took the watch from my hand.

'Give it to me. I like it.'

'I can't, it's my own, from home.'

'You can't? Ah, that's too bad.' He swung his arm and hurled the watch against the brick wall. Then he seated himself calmly back in the shade and tucked his legs under him. 'Hot today, isn't it?'

Without a word I picked up my broken watch and began to whistle. First a foxtrot, then an old tango, then the 'Song of Warsaw' and all the Polish cavalry tunes, and finally the entire repertory of the political left.

But just when I got to the middle of the 'International', I suddenly felt a tall shadow move over me. A heavy hand struck across my back. I turned my head and froze in terror. The Kapo's huge, bloated red face hovered over me, his spade swaying dangerously in mid-air. The stripes of his prison suit stood out sharply against the green of the distant trees. A small red triangle with the numbers 3277 dangled before my eyes, growing more and more enormous.

'What's that you're whistling?' he asked, looking straight into my eyes.

'It's a sort of international song, sir.'

'Do you know the words?'

'Well ... some ... I've heard them a few times,' I said cautiously.

'And have you heard this one?'

And in a hoarse voice he began singing the 'Red Flag'. He let his spade drop, his eyes glistened excitedly. Then he broke off suddenly, picked up the spade and shook his head, half with contempt, half with pity.

'If a real S.S. man'd heard you, you wouldn't be alive right now. But that one over there ... '

The sickly German resting against the brick wall laughed good-naturedly:

'You call this hard labour? You should have been in the Caucasus, like me!'

'Yes, but sir, we've already filled one pond with human bones, and how many more were filled before, and how much was dumped into the Vistula, this neither you nor I know.'

'Enough, you dirty dog!' and he rose from under the wall and looked around for his whip.

'Get your men and go on to dinner,' said the Kapo quickly.

I dropped my spade and vanished around the corner of the incubator. In the distance I could still hear the Kapo's voice, hoarse and asthmatic:

'Yes, yes, the dirty dogs! They should be finished off, every last one of them. You're right, Herr Kommando-führer.'

III

We leave by the road that runs through Harmenz. The tall chestnuts murmur, their shade seems even more green, but somehow drier. Like withered leaves. It is the shade of mid-day.

After emerging on to the road you have to pass a little house with green shutters. Awkward little hearts have been roughly cut out in their centres, and white ruffled curtains are half-drawn over the windows. Under the windows grow delicate, pale roses. A mass of funny little pink flowers peeks out of the window-boxes. On the steps of the veranda, shaded with dark-green ivy, a little girl is playing with a big, sulky dog. The dog, obviously bored, lets her pull him by the ears, and only from time to time shakes his heavy head to chase away the flies. The girl wears a little white dress, her arms are brown and suntanned. The dog is a black Dobermann Pinscher. The girl is the daughter of the Unterscharführer, the boss of Harmenz, and the little house with its little window-boxes and its ruffled curtains is his house.

Before you reach the road, you have to cross over several yards of soft, sticky mud mixed with sawdust and sprinkled with a disinfectant. This is to prevent us from bringing germs into Harmenz. I slip cautiously around the edge of the mess, and we emerge on to the road, where large caldrons of soup have already been set up in a long row. A truck has brought them from the camp. Each Kommando has its own caldrons marked with chalk. I walk around them. We made it on time—no one has yet stolen any of our food.

'These five are ours, good, take them away. The two rows over there belong to the women, hands off. Aha, here's one.' I go on talking loudly, and at the same time drag over a caldron that belongs to the next Kommando, leaving one of ours, only half the size, in its place. I quickly change the chalk marks.

'Take it away!' I boldly shout to the Greeks, who stand eyeing the procedure with total approval.

'Hey you, what d'you think you're doing switching those caldrons? Wait, stop!' yell the men from the other Kommando that has just arrived for dinner, only a little too late.

'Who switched anything? You'd better watch your language, man!'

They start running towards us, but the Greeks quickly draw the caldrons over the ground, groaning, swearing in their own tongue, *putare* and *porka*, shoving and urging each other on, until they disappear beyond the markers that separate the rest of the world from Harmenz. I follow behind. I can still hear the men at the caldrons cursing me up and down, obviously taking a dim view of my entire family, as well as my ancestors. But it is okay: today was my turn, tomorrow will be theirs, first come, first served. Our Kommando patriotism never goes beyond the bounds of sport.

The soup gurgles in the caldrons. The Greeks have set them down on the ground several paces apart and pant heavily, like fish cast upon the sand. With their fingers they eagerly collect the little trickles of sticky hot liquid oozing from under the loosely screwed-on covers. I know how it tastes, that mixture of dust, dirt and sweat from the palm. I carried the caldrons myself not so long ago.

The Greeks stand around in silence and gaze expectantly into my eyes. With a solemn face I walk up to the middle caldron, slowly turn the screw, for one endless half-second keep my hand on the cover and—raise it. The light in the dozen pair of eyes fades suddenly—nettle soup. A thin white fluid gurgles in the caldron, yellow rings of margarine float on the surface. But everybody knows by its colour that on the bottom there are whole, unchopped, stringy nettle stalks which look like rot and stink horribly, and that the soup is the same all the way down: water, water, water ... For a moment the world goes dark before the men's eyes. I replace the cover. We carry the caldrons down the slope without exchanging a word.

Walking in a wide arc, I cross the field to where Ivan's group is tearing up the surface of the meadow by the potato patch. A long row of men in camp stripes stands motionless along a high ridge of black earth. Once in a while a spade moves, someone bends over, freezes for a moment in that position, and then straightens up slowly, shifts the spade and remains for a long time in the half turn, the uncompleted gesture. After a while someone else stirs, swings the spade, and again falls into the same limp stupor. The men do not work with their hands but with their eyes. As soon as an S.S. man or the Kapo appears, the foreman scrambles heavily to his feet, the clatter of the spades grows a bit more lively. But whenever possible, the spades swing up and down empty. The limbs move like those of marionettes—absurd, angular.

I find Ivan inside a sheltered nook. With his pocket-knife he is carving designs in the bark of a thick piece of wood—squares, love knots, little hearts, Ukrainian patterns. An old, trusted Greek kneels beside him, stuffing something inside his bag. I just catch sight of a white feathered wing and the red beak of a goose before Ivan, seeing me come in, throws his coat over the bag. The lard has melted inside my pocket and there is an ugly stain on my trousers.

'From Mrs Haneczka,' I say in a matter-of-fact tone.

'Didn't she send a message? I was supposed to get some eggs.'

'She only asked me to thank you for the soap. She liked it very much.'

'Good. I happened to buy it last night from a Greek Jew in Canada. Gave him three eggs for it.'

Ivan unwraps the lard. It is squashed, soft and yellowish. The very sight of it makes me nauseous, perhaps because I ate too much smoked bacon this morning, and keep tasting it in my mouth.

'Ah, the bitch! Two such fine pieces of soap and this is all she sends? Didn't she give you any cake?' Ivan looks at me suspiciously.

'You're entirely right, Ivan, she didn't give you enough, that's a fact. I've seen the soap ... '

'You have?' He fidgets uneasily. 'Well, I must be going. It's time I gave my men a little shove.'

'Yes, I saw it. She really has given you too little. You deserve more. Especially from me. And you'll get it, I promise you ...'

We look hard into each other's eyes.

IV

There is a mass of tall reeds along one side of the ditch, while the other side is thick with raspberry bushes with pale, dusty leaves. Muddy water runs slowly along the bottom of the ditch, alive with all sorts of green, slimy creatures. Once in a while a black, wriggling eel comes up with the mud—the Greeks always eat it raw.

I stand straddled across the ditch and slowly work my spade over the bottom, at the same time trying to avoid wetting my shoes. The guard, a slow-witted fellow with a small moustache and several triangles on his arm to indicate long service, has walked up to the edge of the ditch and stands watching me in silence.

'And what's that you're making over here?' he asks finally.

'A dyke. And later we'll clean out the ditch, sir.'

'Where did you get such a fine pair of shoes?'

I do, in fact, have good shoes—hand made, with a double sole and ingeniously punched holes, Hungarian style. My friends brought them from the loading ramp.

'I got them here at the camp, and this shirt, too,' I explain, showing him my silk shirt which cost me a pound of tomatoes.

'So you get shoes like that? Just look at what I've got to wear,' and he points to his worn-out, cracked boots with a patch on the right toe. I nod sympathetically.

'Listen, how about selling me yours?'

I throw him a look of utter amazement.

'But how can I sell you camp property? How can I?'

He rests his rifle against the bench, walks up closer and leans over the water in which he can see his own reflection. I reach down and splash it around with my spade.

'As long as nobody knows, it's all right. I'll give you bread, I've got some in my sack.'

Last week alone I received sixteen loaves of bread from Warsaw. Besides, a pair of shoes like mine is good for at least a litre of vodka. Therefore I merely smile at him politely.

'Thank you, but we get such good rations in the camp that I'm not hungry. I have enough bread and lard. But if you, sir, have too much, why don't you give it to the Jews working over there by the embankment? The one, for example, that's carrying the turf,' I say, pointing to the skinny little Jew with red, watery eyes. 'He's a very decent fellow. Anyway, my shoes aren't all that good, the sole is coming off.' I have, it is true, a crack in my sole. Sometimes I hide a few dollars there, sometimes a few marks, sometimes a letter. The guard bites his lip and gazes at me from under knitted brows.

'What did they lock you up for?' he asks.

'I was walking along the street—there was a round-up. They nabbed me, locked me up, brought me here. For no reason.'

'That's what all of you say.'

'No, sir, not all. A friend of mine was arrested for singing out of tune. You know, *falsch gesungen.*'

The spade which I drag uninterruptedly over the bottom of the slimy ditch comes up against something hard. I tear at it. A piece of wire. I curse under my breath. The guard continues to stare at me, dumbfounded.

'*Was, falsch gesungen?*'

'Well, it's a long story. Once, during a church service in Warsaw, when everyone was singing hymns, my friend started singing the national anthem. But since he sang

65

out of tune, they locked him up. And they said they wouldn't let him out until he learned to sing properly. They even beat him regularly, but it was no use. I'm sure he won't get out before the war is over, because he's quite unmusical. Once he even confused a German march with Chopin's "Funeral March"!'

The guard hissed through his teeth and walked back to his bench. He sat down, picked up his rifle and, playing absent-mindedly with the bolt, went through the motions of loading and firing. Then he suddenly raised his head, as if remembering something.

'You! Come over here! I'll let you have the bread if you go and give it to the Jews yourself,' he said, reaching for his sack.

I smiled as politely as I could.

Along the other side of the ditch runs the line of sentries, and the guards have orders to fire on sight at any prisoner who crossed into the zone beyond it. For every head they get three day's furlough and five marks.

'Unfortunately, I'm not allowed to. But if you wish, sir, you may throw the bread over. I'll catch it, I really will.'

I stand waiting, but all of a sudden the guard drops the sack to the ground, jumps to his feet, and salutes. The Rottenführer is passing along the road.

Janek—a young, charming native son of Warsaw, who understands nothing of the ways of the camp and probably never will—was working diligently at my side, shovelling the mud and the sand and piling it neatly alongside the ditch, almost directly at the guard's feet. The Rottenführer approached and looked at us in the way one looks at a pair of horses drawing a cart, or cattle grazing in the field. Janek threw him a broad, friendly, man-to-man smile.

'We're cleaning out the ditch, sir, it certainly is full of mud.'

The Rottenführer started and eyed the speaking prisoner with utter astonishment.

'Come here!' he said.

Janek put down his spade, jumped over the ditch, and walked up to him. The Rottenführer raised his hand and slammed him across the face with all his strength. Janek staggered, clutched at the raspberry bushes, and slid down into the slime. The water gurgled and I began to choke with laughter.

'I don't give a damn what you might be doing in the ditch! You can do nothing for all I care. But when you're addressing an S.S. man, take off your cap and stand to attention,' said the Rottenführer and walked off. I helped Janek scramble out of the mud.

'What did I get that for, what, in the name of heaven?' he asked in amazement, utterly confused.

'Next time, don't volunteer,' I said, 'and now go and wash.'

Just as we were finishing cleaning out the ditch, the Kapo's boy arrived. I reached for my sack. I moved aside a loaf of bread, a piece of lard and an onion. I took out a lemon. The guard observed me in silence from across the ditch.

'Here boy, take this for your Kapo,' I said.

'Okay, Tadek. And listen, how about something to eat? You know, something sweet. Or a few eggs. No, no, I'm not hungry. I ate at the house. Mrs Haneczka made me some scrambled eggs. What a woman! Except that she's always asking about Ivan. But you see, when the Kapo goes over there they never give him anything.'

'If he stopped beating people, maybe they would.'

'You tell him that.'

'And what has he got you for? Don't you know how to "organize" things? If you're smart and keep your eyes open, you'll see that some of the men catch geese and then fry them in the barracks at night, while your Kapo has to eat soup. By the way, how did he enjoy the nettles?'

The boy listens attentively with a knowing smile on his face. He is young but quite clever. Though only sixteen, he has already served in the German army, and has done quite a lot of smuggling besides.

'Let me have it straight, Tadek. After all, we know each other well. Who are you putting me on to?'

I shrug my shoulders.

'Nobody. But you take a good look at the geese.'

'Do you know that another disappeared yesterday, and the Unterscharführer whipped the Kapo and was so furious he also took his watch? Well, I'll be going, and I promise to keep my eyes open.'

We walk back together, since it is time for dinner. Piercing whistles come from the direction of the caldrons. The men drop their tools wherever they happen to be standing. Abandoned spades stick out on the embankment in rows. Exhausted prisoners from all over the field drag themselves slowly towards the caldrons, trying to stretch out the blessed moment just before dinner, to relish the hunger which they will shortly satisfy. Ivan's group is last, for Ivan has stopped by the ditch and talks a long time to 'my' guard. The guard points his hand, Ivan nods. But shouts and calls urge him away. As he walks by, he flings at me:

'Didn't get much accomplished, did you?'

'The day is still young,' I retort.

He throws me a challenging sidelong glance.

V

Inside the empty incubator the Kapo's boy is setting out the dishes, wiping the benches and preparing the table for dinner. The Kommando clerk, a Greek linguist, huddles in one corner, trying to make himself as small and inconspicuous as possible. Through the wide-open doors we can see his face, the colour of a boiled lobster, and his eyes, watery as frog-spawn. Outside, in a little courtyard encircled by a high ridge of earth, the prisoners are gathered. They have sat down in formation, exactly as they were standing, lined up five in a row, arranged in groups. Their legs are crossed, their bodies erect, their hands down along their thighs. While dinner is being served nobody is allowed to move a muscle. Afterwards, they will be permitted to lean back and rest against the knees of the man behind, but never, never to break formation. Over to the left, under the shade of the ridge, sit the S.S. guards. Relaxed, their revolvers lying across their knees, they take slices of bread from their sacks, carefully spread them with margarine and eat slowly, savouring each mouthful. Beside one of them squats Rubin, a Jew from 'Canada'. They talk in whispers. It is strictly business, partly for Rubin, partly for the Kapo. The Kapo himself, huge and red-faced, stands over by the caldron.

We run around with bowls in our hands, like highly skilled waiters. In complete silence we serve the soup, in complete silence we wrest the bowls out of hands that still try desperately to scrape up some food from the empty bottom, wanting to prolong the moment of eating, to take a last drop, to run a finger over the edge. Suddenly the Kapo plunges between the ranks—he has spotted a man licking his bowl. He pushes him in the face, throwing him over, kicks him time and again in the genitals, and then goes off, stepping over arms, knees, faces, taking care to avoid those who are still eating.

All eyes look eagerly into the Kapo's face. There are two more caldrons—second helpings. Each day the Kapo relishes this particular moment. The many years spent at the camp entitle him to the absolute power he has over the men. With the end of his ladle he points out the chosen few who merit a second helping. He never makes a mistake. The second helping is for those who work better, for the stronger, the healthier. The sick, the weaklings, the emaciated, have no right to an extra bowl of water with nettles. Food must not be wasted on people who are about to go to the gas chamber.

The foremen, by virtue of their office, are entitled to two full bowls of soup with potatoes and meat scooped up from the bottom of the caldron. Holding my bowl in my hand I glance around me, undecided. I can feel someone's intent stare fixed on me. In the first row sits Becker, his bulging, hungry eyes glued to the soup.

'Here, take it, maybe you'll choke on it.'

Without a word he seizes the bowl from my hand and eats greedily.

'Be sure to set the plate down beside you for the Kapo's boy to collect; don't let the Kapo see it.'

I give my second bowl to Andrei. In return he will bring me apples. He works in the orchard.

'Rubin, what news did you hear from the guard?' I ask in an undertone as I walk past him to get in the shade.

'He says they've occupied Kiev,' he whispers.

I stop, astonished. He waves me on impatiently. I walk to the shade, fold my coat under me so as not to soil my silk shirt, and stretch out comfortably. This is a time to rest, every man as best he can.

The Kapo, having eaten two bowls of soup, went to the incubator to doze off. Then his boy drew a slice of boiled meat out of his pocket, cut it up on bread, and proceeded to eat solemnly before the eyes of the hungry crowd, taking an occasional bite at an onion, crunching it like an apple. The men have stretched out in tight rows, one behind the other, and, covering their faces with their coats, have dropped off into a heavy but restless sleep.

Andrei and I lie in the shade. A short distance away we can see girls with white kerchiefs on their heads—a women's Kommando has settled down near by. The girls wave, giggle, and try to attract our attention. A few of us wave back. At the edge of the courtyard, one girl is on her knees, holding a large, heavy beam extended above her head. Every minute or so, the S.S. man guarding the Kommando slackens the leash of his dog. The dog leaps up to the girl's face, barking furiously.

'A thief?' I wonder lazily, turning to Andrei.

'No, they caught her in the corn with Petro. Petro ran away,' he says.

'Can she hold it for five minutes?'

'She can. She's a strong girl.'

She did not. Her arms sagged, the beam tumbled down, and she fell forward on the dirt, breaking into loud sobs. Andrei turned away and looked at me.

'You haven't got a cigarette, have you? Too bad. Ah, life!' He wrapped his coat around his head, stretched out, and fell asleep. I too was getting ready to doze off when the Kapo's boy tugged at my sleeve.

'Kapo wants you. But watch your step, he's really mad.'

The Kapo has just awakened, his eyes are red. He rubs them, staring fixedly into space.

'You!' He presses his finger to my chest. 'Why did you give your soup away?'

'I've got other food.'

'What did he give you in exchange?'

'Nothing.'

He shakes his head in disbelief. His enormous jaws work, like those of a cow chewing the cud.

'Tomorrow you won't get any soup at all. It is for those who have nothing else to eat. Understand?'

'All right, Kapo.'

'Why haven't you made the four stretchers, the way I told you? Did you forget?'

'I haven't had time. You saw what I was doing all morning.'

'You'll make them this afternoon. And watch out, or you'll end up on one of them yourself. I can fix that, believe me.'

'May I go now?'

Only then did he look directly into my face. He fixed on me the lifeless, vacant stare of a man torn out of profound contemplation.

'Why are you still here?' he asked.

VI

From beneath the chestnut trees growing along the road came a stifled cry. I collected my wrenches and screws, arranged the stretchers one on top of the other, and called:

'Janek, don't forget the box, and be a good boy!' and I rushed to the road.

There, on the ground, lay Becker, moaning and spitting blood. Ivan stood over him, blindly kicking his face, his back, his belly ...

'Look what he's done! Gobbled up all of your dinner, the thieving swine!'

Mrs Haneczka's tin bowl with some mush still left on the bottom was lying in the dirt. Becker's face was smeared with mush all over.

'I shoved his ugly mug right in it,' said Ivan, panting heavily. 'There, he's all yours, I've got to go.'

I turned to Becker. 'Wash out the bowl and set it under the tree. And watch out for the Kapo. I've just finished making four stretchers. You know what that means, don't you?'

On the road Andrei is teaching two Greek Jews to march.
They do not know how. The Kapo has already broken two
whips over their heads and warned them that they must
learn, or else ... Andrei tied a stick to each of their legs and
tries his best to explain: 'You no good bastard, can't you
understand what's left, what's right? *Links, links!*' The
terrified Greeks, their eyes popping, march round and
round in a circle shuffling their feet along the gravel. A
huge cloud of dust rises in the air. By the ditch, next to the
guard who wanted my shoes, several friends of mine are
busily 'arranging' the earth. They pat it down gently and
smooth it over with the backs of their spades, like dough.
As I walk past them on my way to the other end of the
field, leaving deep tracks in the soft earth, they call
loudly:
'Hey, Tadek, what's new?'
'Not much, they've taken Kiev!'
'Is that really true?'
'What a silly question!'
Shouting back and forth I pass them and continue on
along the ditch. Suddenly I hear someone scream after
me:
'Halt, halt, du Warschauer!'
Running behind me along the other side of the ditch is
'my' guard, his rifle aimed. 'Stop, stop!'
I stop. The guard fights his way through the raspberry
bushes, loudly cocks his rifle.
'What's that you just said? About Kiev? So, now you're
spreading political rumours! So, you've got a secret organization! Number, number, let's have your serial number!'
Shaking with fury and indignation he holds out a scrap
of paper, nervously searches for a pencil. I feel an emptiness in the pit of my stomach, but I recover quickly.
'Excuse me, sir, but I think you misunderstood. Your

Polish is not too good. I was speaking of the sticks* Andrei tied to the feet of the Greeks, over there on the road. I was saying how funny they looked.'

'That's right, that's exactly what he was saying.' The men who have gathered around us nod in agreement.

The guard swings the butt of his rifle, as if trying to hit me from across the ditch.

'You, you! ... I'm going to report you to the political section today! Come on, what's your number?'

'One hundred and nineteen, one hundred and ...'

'Let's see your arm!'

'Here.' I hold out my forearm with the number tattooed on it, feeling certain he cannot read it at that distance.

'Come closer!'

'That's *verboten*. You may report me if you like, but I'm not as stupid as "White Vaska".'

A few days ago White Vaska climbed up a birch tree growing along the sentry line to cut some twigs for a broom. In the camp, a broom like that may be exchanged for bread or soup. A guard took aim and fired, a bullet passed sideways through Vaska's chest and came out in the back between his shoulder blades. We carried the boy's body back to camp.

I walk away feeling angry. Around the bend of the road, Rubin catches up with me.

'See what you've done? Now what's going to happen?'

'Why should anything happen?'

'Ah, but you'll tell them you got it from me ... Oi, what a fine thing you did! How could you've shouted so loud? You're out to ruin me, Tadek!'

'What are you scared of? Our people don't sing.'

'Yes, I know it, and you know it, but *sicher ist sicher*. Better to be on the safe side. Listen, how about letting

* An untranslatable play on words. The Polish word for stick is pronounced almost the same as Kiev.

74

the guard have your shoes? I guarantee he'll co-operate.
I'll try talking to him myself, see? For you I'll do it. He
and I have done business before.'

'Great, now I'll also have that to tell them about you,
Rubin.'

'Our future looks black, Tadek ... Better let him have
the shoes, and I'll settle the details with him later. He's
not a bad guy.'

'Only he's lived too long. I intend to keep my shoes,
because I like them. But I have a watch. It isn't running,
and the glass is broken, but then, what have I got you
for? You're a clever man, Rubin. In fact, you can give him
your own watch, it didn't cost you anything.'

'Oi, Tadek, Tadek ...'

Rubin stashes away my watch. In the distance I hear a
shout:

'Hey, railwayman!'

I rush across the field. The Kapo's eyes glisten dangerously; there are traces of foam around the corners of his
mouth. His hands, his enormous gorilla hands, sway back
and forth, his fingers twitch nervously.

'What were you trading with Rubin?'

'But didn't you see, Kapo? You always see everything. I
gave him my watch.'

'Whaat?' Slowly his hands begin to move towards my
throat.

Without making the slightest move (he is a wild beast, I
suddenly thought), without shifting my eyes from his face,
I burst out in one breath:

'I gave him my watch because the guard wants to report
me to the political section for subversive activities.'

The Kapo's hands relaxed slowly and dropped to his
sides. His jaw hung loose, like an old dog's. He rocked the
spade to and fro, undecided.

'Go back to work. And watch out or they'll be carrying

you back to camp on one of those stretchers of yours ... '

At that moment he suddenly stiffened to attention and tore his cap off his head. I threw myself to one side, struck in the rear by a bicycle. I removed my cap. The Unterscharführer, the boss of all Harmenz, hopped off the bicycle, his face red and excited.

'What's the matter with this crazy Kommando? Why are your men over there walking around with sticks tied to their feet? Why aren't they working?'

'They're learning how to march, sir.'

'They can't march? Then kill them! Did you hear, by the way, that another goose has disappeared?'

'Why are you standing here like a stupid oaf?' snarled the Kapo, turning to me. 'You heard the Unterscharführer! Go and tell Andrei to take care of them. *Los!*'

I flew down the path.

'Finish them off, Andrei! Kapo's orders!'

Andrei seized a stick and struck out at random. The Greek covered his head with his arm, let out a howl, and fell. Andrei laid the stick across the man's throat, stood up on the two ends, and began to rock. I walked away quickly.

In the distance I see that the Kapo and the S.S. man have gone over to talk to my guard. The Kapo gesticulates violently, shaking his spade; his cap is down over his eyes. Then they walk away and in turn Rubin approaches the guard. The guard rises from the bench, draws close to the ditch and finally steps on to the dyke. In a little while Rubin nods to me.

'Come and thank Mr Guard for not reporting you.'

Rubin is no longer wearing my watch.

I thank the guard and return to work. The old Greek, Ivan's confidant, stops me along the way.

'*Camarade, camarade,* that S.S. man came from the main camp, didn't he?'

76

'Where else?'

'Then it's really true about the selection!' and the withered, silver-haired old merchant from Salonica throws his spade aside and lifts up his arms, as though in a trance:

'*Nous sommes des hommes misérables, O Dieu, Dieu!*'

His pale-blue eyes gaze up into the equally pale and blue sky.

VII

We hoist up the little cart. Filled to the brim with sand, it has gone off the rails right at the turntable. Four pairs of bony arms push it backwards and forwards, rock it. We put it in motion, raise the front wheels, set them back on to the rails. Now we work a wedge underneath, but just when the cart is almost back on the rails we suddenly let go and straighten up.

'*Antreten!*' I scream, and blow my whistle.

The cart falls back heavily, its wheels dig into the earth. Someone tosses the wedge to the side; we pour the sand from the cart straight over the turntable. After all, it can be cleared away tomorrow.

Antreten. Only after a moment or two do we realize it is much too early. The sun still stands high above our heads, quite a distance from the tree crowns which it usually reaches by *Antreten* time. It cannot be later than three o'clock. The men look puzzled and anxious. We line up, five in a row, close ranks, straighten our backs, tighten our belts.

The camp clerk counts us over and over.

The S.S. men and the Kommando guards arrive from the direction of the house and form a ring around us. We stand motionless. In the rear of the Kommando several men are carrying two stretchers with two corpses.

Along the road there is more activity than usual. The

people of Harmenz walk to and fro, disturbed by our early departure. But to the seasoned camp inmates the situation seems clear—there will, indeed, be a selection.

Several times already we caught sight of Mrs Haneczka's bright kerchief in the vicinity, but then it disappeared. Now she is back. Her questioning eyes glide over our faces. Setting her basket down on the ground, she leans against the barn and looks around. I follow the direction of her gaze. She is looking anxiously at Ivan.

The Kapo and the sickly Kommandoführer have arrived right behind the S.S. men.

'Spread out in open order and put up your hands,' says the Kapo.

Now we understand: we are to be searched. We unfasten our coats, open up our sacks. The guard is swift and efficient. He runs his hands over your body, reaches inside your sack. In addition to several onions, some old bacon and what is left of my bread, he finds apples, obviously from our orchard.

'Where'd you get these?'

I raise my head—it is 'my' guard.

'From a parcel, sir.'

He looks me in the eyes with an ironic smile.

'I ate the very same kind this morning.'

They disbowel our pockets, pull out corn cobs, herbs, seeds, apples, chunks of sunflower; now and then there is an abrupt scream: someone is being beaten up.

Suddenly the Unterscharführer pushed his way into the middle of the ranks and dragged aside Ivan's old Greek who was clutching a large, well-stuffed sack.

'Open it!' he snapped.

With trembling hands the Greek untied the rope. The Unterscharführer looked inside and called to the Kapo:

'Look Kapo, here's our goose!'

And he drew out of the sack a big bird with enormous,

wide-spread wings. The Kapo's boy, who had also rushed over, shouted triumphantly:

'Here it is, here it is, didn't I tell you?'

The Kapo raised his whip, ready to strike.

'Don't,' said the S.S. man, stopping him. He drew a revolver out of his holster and, waving the weapon eloquently, turned to face the Greek.

'Where did you get it? If you won't answer I'll shoot you.'

The Greek was silent. The S.S. man raised the revolver. I glanced at Ivan. His face was absolutely white. Our eyes met. He tightened his lips and stepped forward. He walked up to the S.S. man, took off his cap, and said:

'I gave it to him.'

All eyes were fixed on Ivan. The Unterscharführer slowly raised the whip and struck him across the face, once, twice, three times. Then he began to strike his head. The whip hissed. Deep, bloody gashes stood out on Ivan's face, but he did not fall. He stood erect, hat in hand, his arms straight against his sides. He made no attempt to avoid the blows, but only swayed imperceptibly on his feet.

The Unterscharführer let his hand drop.

'Take his serial number and make up a report. Kommando—dismissed!'

We marched off at an even, military pace, leaving behind a heap of sunflower heads, weeds, rags, and crushed apples, and on top a large, red-beaked goose with tremendous wide-spread wings. In the rear of the Kommando walked Ivan, supported by no one. Behind him, on stretchers, we carried two corpses covered with branches.

As we passed Mrs Haneczka, I turned to look at her. She stood pale and straight, her hands pressed over her breast. Her lips quivered nervously. She raised her head and looked at me. Then I saw that her large black eyes were filled with tears.

After roll-call we were driven into the barracks. We lay

on the bunks, peered through the cracks in the walls, and
waited for the selection to come to an end.

'I feel as if this damn selection were somehow my
fault. What a curious power words have ... Here in Auschwitz even evil words seem to materialize.'

'Take it easy,' said Kazik. 'Instead, let me have something to go with this sausage.'

'Don't you have any tomatoes?'

'You must be kidding!'

I pushed aside the sandwiches he had made.

'I can't eat.'

Outside, the selection was almost finished. The S.S. doctor, having taken the serial numbers and noted the total
of the men selected, went on to the next barracks. Kazik was
getting ready to leave.

'I'm off to try and find some cigarettes. But you know,
Tadek, you're really a sucker. If anyone'd eaten up my
mush, I'd have made mincemeat of him.'

At that moment, a large grey head emerged from below,
and a pair of blinking, guilty eyes gazed up at us over the
edge of the bunk. It was Becker, his face exhausted and
somehow even older-looking.

'Tadek, I want to ask a favour of you.'

'Go ahead,' I said, leaning down to him.

'Tadek, I'm going to the cremo.'

I leaned over still more and peered into his eyes—they
were calm and empty.

'Tadek, I've been so hungry for such a long time. Give
me something to eat. Just this last time.'

'Do you know this Jew?' asked Kazik, tapping my knee.

'It's Becker,' I answered in a whisper. 'Okay, Jew, come
on up and eat. And when you've had enough, take the rest
with you to the cremo. Climb up. I don't sleep here anyway,
so I don't mind your lice.'

'Tadek,' Kazik pulled at my arm, 'come with me. I've

got a wonderful apple cake at my place, straight from home.'

As he scrambled down, he nudged me.

'Look,' he whispered.

I looked at Becker. His eyes were half-closed and, like a blind man, he was vainly groping with his hand for the board to pull himself on to the bunk.

The People
Who Walked On

It was early spring when we began building a soccer
field on the broad clearing behind the hospital barracks.
The location was excellent: the gypsies to the left, with
their roaming children, their lovely, trim nurses, and
their women sitting by the hour in the latrines; to the
rear—a barbed-wire fence, and behind it the loading ramp
with the wide railway tracks and the endless coming and
going of trains; and beyond the ramp, the women's camp—
Frauen Konzentration Lager. No one, of course, ever called
it by its full name. We simply said F.K.L.—that was enough.
To the right of the field were the crematoria, some of them
at the back of the ramp, next to the F.K.L., others even
closer, right by the fence. Sturdy buildings that sat solidly
on the ground. And in front of the crematoria, a small wood
which had to be crossed on the way to the gas.

We worked on the soccer field throughout the spring,
and before it was finished we started planting flowers under
the barracks windows and decorating the blocks with intri-

cate zigzag designs made of crushed red brick. We planted spinach and lettuce, sunflowers and garlic. We laid little green lawns with grass transplanted from the edges of the soccer field, and sprinkled them daily with water brought in barrels from the lavatories.

Just when the flowers were about to bloom, we finished the soccer field.

From then on, the flowers were abandoned, the sick lay by themselves in the hospital beds, and we played soccer. Every day, as soon as the evening meal was over, anybody who felt like it came to the field and kicked the ball around. Others stood in clusters by the fence and talked across the entire length of the camp with the girls from the F.K.L.

One day I was goalkeeper. As always on Sundays, a sizeable crowd of hospital orderlies and convalescent patients had gathered to watch the game. Keeping goal, I had my back to the ramp. The ball went out and rolled all the way to the fence. I ran after it, and as I reached to pick it up, I happened to glance at the ramp.

A train had just arrived. People were emerging from the cattle cars and walking in the direction of the little wood. All I could see from where I stood were bright splashes of colour. The women, it seemed, were already wearing summer dresses; it was the first time that season. The men had taken off their coats, and their white shirts stood out sharply against the green of the trees. The procession moved along slowly, growing in size as more and more people poured from the freight cars. And then it stopped. The people sat down on the grass and gazed in our direction. I returned with the ball and kicked it back inside the field. It travelled from one foot to another and, in a wide arc, returned to the goal. I kicked it towards a corner. Again it rolled out into the grass. Once more I ran to retrieve it. But as I reached down, I stopped in amazement—the ramp was empty. Out of the whole colourful summer procession, not one person remained. The train too was gone. Again the F.K.L. blocks were in unobstructed view, and again the orderlies and the patients stood along the barbed-wire fence calling to the girls, and the girls answered them across the ramp.

Between two throw-ins in a soccer game, right behind my back, three thousand people had been put to death.

In the following months, the processions to the little wood moved along two roads: one leading straight from the ramp, the other past the hospital wall. Both led to the crematoria, but some of the people had the good fortune to walk beyond them, all the way to the Zauna, and this meant more than just a bath and a delousing, a barber's shop and a new prison suit. It meant staying alive. In a concentration camp, true, but—alive.

Each day, as I got up in the morning to scrub the hospital floors, the people were walking—along both roads. Women, men, children. They carried their bundles.

When I sat down to dinner—and not a bad one, either—the people were walking. Our block was bathed in sunlight; we threw the doors and the windows wide open and sprinkled the floors with water to keep the dust down. In the afternoons I delivered packages which had been brought that morning from the Auschwitz post office. The clerk distributed mail. The doctors dressed wounds and gave injections. There was, as a matter of fact, only one hypodermic needle for the entire block. On warm evenings I sat at the barracks door reading *Mon frère Yves* by Pierre Loti—while the procession continued on and on, along both roads.

Often, in the middle of the night, I walked outside; the lamps glowed in the darkness above the barbed-wire fences. The roads were completely black, but I could distinctly hear the far-away hum of a thousand voices—the procession moved on and on. And then the entire sky would light up; there would be a burst of flame above the wood ... and terrible human screams.

I stared into the night, numb, speechless, frozen with horror. My entire body trembled and rebelled, somehow even without my participation. I no longer controlled my body, although I could feel its every tremor. My mind was completely calm, only the body seemed to revolt.

Soon afterwards, I left the hospital. The days were filled with important events. The Allied Armies had landed on the shores of France. The Russian front, we heard, had started to move west towards Warsaw.

But in Birkenau, day and night long lines of trains loaded with people waited at the station. The doors were unsealed, the people started walking—along both roads.

Located next to the camp's labour sector was the deserted, unfinished Sector C. Here, only the barracks and the high voltage fence around them had been completed. The roofs, however, were not yet covered with tar sheets, and some of the blocks still had no bunks. An average Birkenau block, furnished with three tiers of bunks, could hold up to five hundred people. But every block in Sector C was now being packed with a thousand or more young women picked from among the people on the ramp ... Twenty-eight blocks—over thirty thousand women. Their heads were shaved and they were issued little sleeveless summer dresses. But they were not given underwear. Nor spoons, nor bowls, nor even a rag to clean themselves with. Birkenau was situated on marshes, at the foot of a mountain range. During the day, the air was warm and so transparent that the mountains were in clear view, but in the morning they lay shrouded in a thick, icy mist. The mornings were cold and penetrating. For us, this meant merely a refreshing pause before a hot summer day, but the women, who only twenty yards to our right had been standing at roll-call since five in the morning, turned blue from the cold and huddled together like a flock of partridges.

We named the camp—Persian Market. On sunny, warm days the women would emerge from the barracks and mill around in the wide aisles between the blocks. Their bright summer dresses and the gay kerchiefs on their shaved heads created the atmosphere of a busy, colourful market—a Persian Market because of its exotic character.

From afar, the women were faceless and ageless. Nothing more than white blotches and pastel figures.

The Persian Market was not yet completed. The Wagner Kommando began building a road through the sector, packing it down with a heavy roller. Others fiddled around with the plumbing and worked on the washrooms that were to be installed throughout all the sectors of Birkenau. Still others were busy stocking up the Persian Market with the camp's basic equipment—supplies of blankets, metal cups and spoons—which they arranged carefully in the warehouses under the direction of the chief supervisor, the assigned S.S. officer. Naturally, much of the stuff evaporated immediately, expertly 'organized' by the men working on the job.

My comrades and I laid a roof over the shack of every Block Elder in the Persian Market. It was not done on official order, nor did we work out of charity. Neither did we do it out of a feeling of solidarity with the old serial numbers, the F.K.L. women who had been placed there in all the responsible posts. In fact, we used 'organized' tar-boards and melted 'organized' tar, and for every roll of tar-board, every bucket of tar, an Elder had to pay. She had to pay the Kapo, the Kommandoführer, the Kommando 'bigwigs'. She could pay in various ways: with gold, food, the women of her block, or with her own body. It depended.

On a similar basis, the electricians installed electricity, the carpenters built and furnished the shacks, using 'organized' lumber, the masons provided metal stoves and cemented them in place.

It was at that time that I came to know the anatomy of this strange camp. We would arrive there in the morning, pushing a cart loaded with tar-sheets and tar. At the gate stood the S.S. women-guards, hippy blondes in black leather boots. They searched us and let us in. Then they themselves went to inspect the blocks. Not infrequently they had lovers among the masons and carpenters. They slept with them in the unfinished washrooms or the Block Elders' shacks.

We would push our cart into the camp, between the barracks, and there, on some little square, would light a fire and melt the tar. A crowd of women would immediately surround us. They begged us to give them anything, a penknife, a handkerchief, a spoon, a pencil, a piece of paper, a shoe string, or bread.

'Listen, you can always manage somehow,' they would say. 'You've been in the camp a long time and you've survived. Surely you have all you need. Why won't you share it with us?'

At first we gave them everything we happened to have with us, and then turned our pockets inside out to show we had nothing more. We took off our shirts and handed them over. But gradually we began coming with empty pockets and gave them nothing.

These women were not so much alike as it had seemed when we looked at them from another sector, from a distance of twenty metres.

Among them were small girls, whose hair had not been shaved, stray little cherubs from a painting of the Last Judgment. There were young girls who gazed with surprise at the women crowding around us, and who looked at us, coarse, brutal men, with contempt. Then there were married women, who desperately begged for news of their lost husbands, and mothers trying to find a trace of their children.

'We are so miserable, so cold, so hungry,' they cried. 'Tell us, are they at least a little bit better off?'

'They are, if God is just,' we would answer solemnly, without the usual mocking and teasing.

'Surely they're not dead?' the women asked, looking searchingly into our faces.

We would walk away without a word, eager to get back to work.

The majority of the Block Elders at the Persian Market were Slovak girls who managed to communicate in the the language of the new inmates. Every one of these girls had behind her several years of concentration camp. Every one of them remembered the early days of the F.K.L., when female corpses piled up along the barracks walls and rotted, unremoved, in hospital beds—and when human excrement grew into monstrous heaps inside the blocks.

Despite their rough manner, they had retained their femininity and human kindness. Probably they too had their lovers, and probably they too stole margarine and tins of food in order to pay for blankets and dresses, but ...

... but I remember Mirka, a short, stocky 'pink' girl. Her shack was all done up in pink too, with pink ruffled curtains across the window that faced the block. The pink light inside the shack set a pink glow over the girl's face, making her look as if she were wrapped in a delicate misty veil. There was a Jew in our Kommando with very bad teeth who was in love with Mirka. He was always running around the camp trying to buy fresh eggs for her, and then throwing them, protected in soft wrapping, over the barbed-wire fence. He would spend many long hours with her, paying little attention to the S.S. women inspecting the barracks or to our chief who made his rounds with a tremendous revolver hanging from his white summer uniform.

One day Mirka came running over to where several of us were laying a roof. She signalled frantically to the Jew and called, turning to me:

'Please come down! Maybe you can help too!'

We slid off the roof and down the barracks door. Mirka grabbed us by the hands and pulled us in the direction of her shack. There she led us between the cots and pointing to a mass of colourful quilts and blankets on top of which lay a child, she said breathlessy:

'Look, it's dying! Tell me, what can I do? What could have made it so sick so suddenly?'

The child was asleep, but very restless. It looked like a rose in a golden frame—its burning cheeks were surrounded by a halo of blond hair.

'What a pretty child,' I whispered.

'Pretty!' cried Mirka. 'All you know is that it's pretty! But it can die any moment! I've had to hide it so they wouldn't take it to the gas! What if an S.S. woman finds it? Help me!'

The Jew put his arm around her shoulders. She pushed him away and suddenly burst into sobs. I shrugged, turned around, and left the barracks.

In the distance, I could see trains moving along the ramp. They were bringing new people who would walk in the direction of the little wood. One Canada group was just returning from the ramp, and along the wide camp road passed another Canada group going to take its place. Smoke was rising above the treetops. I seated myself next to the boiling bucket of tar and, stirring it slowly, sat thinking for a long time. At one point a wild thought suddenly shot across my mind: I too would like to have a child with rose-coloured cheeks and light blond hair I laughed aloud at such a ridiculous notion and climbed up on the roof to lay the hot tar.

And I remember another Block Elder, a big redhead with broad feet and chapped hands. She did not have a separate shack, only a few blankets spread over the bed and instead of walls a few other blankets thrown across a piece of rope.

'I mustn't make them feel,' she would say, pointing to the women packed tightly in the bunks, 'that I want to cut myself off from them. Maybe I can't give them anything, but I won't take anything away from them either.'

'Do you believe in life after death?' she asked me once in the middle of some lighthearted conversation.

'Sometimes,' I answered cautiously. 'Once I believed in it when I was in jail, and again once when I came close to dying here in the camp.'

'But if a man does evil, he'll be punished, won't he?'

'I suppose so, unless there are some criteria of justice other than the man-made criteria. You know ... the kind that explain causes and motivations, and erase guilt by making it appear insignificant in the light of the overall harmony of the universe. Can a crime committed on one level be punishable on a different one?'

'But I mean in a normal, human sense!' she exclaimed. 'It ought to be punished. No question about it.'

'And you, would you do good if you were able to?'

'I seek no rewards. I build roofs and want to survive the concentration camp.'

'But do you think that they', she pointed with her chin in an indefinite direction, 'can go unpunished?'

'I think that for those who have suffered unjustly, justice alone is not enough. They want the guilty to suffer unjustly too. Only this will they understand as justice.'

'You're a pretty smart fellow! But you wouldn't have the slightest idea how to divide bread justly, without giving more to your own mistress!' she said bitterly and walked into the block. The women were lying in the rows of bunks, head to head. Their faces were still, only the eyes seemed alive, large and shining. Hunger had already started in this part of the camp. The redheaded Elder moved from bunk to bunk, talking to the women to distract them from their thoughts. She pulled out the singers and told them to sing, the dancers—and told them to dance, the poets—and made them recite poetry.

'All the time, endlessly, they ask me about their mothers, their fathers. They beg me to write to them.'

'They've asked me too. It's just too bad.'

'Ah, you! You come and then you go, but me? I plead with them, I beg them—if anyone is pregnant, don't report to the doctor, if anyone is sick, stay in the barracks! But do you think they believe me? It's no good, no matter how hard you try to protect them. What can you do if they fall all over themselves to get to the gas?'

One of the girls was standing on top of a table singing a popular tune. When she finished, the women in the bunks began to applaud. The girl bowed, smiling. The redheaded Elder covered her face with her rough hands.

'I can't stand it any longer! It's too disgusting!' she whispered. And suddenly she jumped up and rushed over to the table. 'Get down!' she screamed at the singer.

The women fell silent. She raised her arm.

'Quiet!' she shouted, though nobody spoke a word. 'You've been asking me about your parents and your children. I haven't told you, I felt sorry for you. But now I'll tell you, so that you know, because they'll do the same with you if you get sick! Your children, your husbands and your parents are not in another camp at all. They've been stuffed into a room and gassed! Gassed, do you understand? Like millions of others, like my own mother and father. They're burning in deep pits and in ovens ... The smoke which you see above the rooftops doesn't come from the brick plant at all, as you're being told. It's smoke from your children! Now go on and sing.' She finished calmly, pointing her finger at the terrified singer. Then she turned around and walked out of the barracks.

It was undeniable that the conditions in both Auschwitz and Birkenau were steadily improving. At the beginning, beating and killing were the rule, but later this became only sporadic. At first, you had to sleep on the floor lying on your side because of the lack of space, and could turn over only on command; later you slept in bunks, or where-ever you wished, sometimes even in bed. Originally, you had to stand at roll-call for as long as two days at a time, later—only until the second gong, until nine o'clock. In the early years, packages were forbidden, later you could receive 500 grams, and finally as much as you wanted. Pockets of any kind were at first strictly taboo, but eventually even civilian clothes could sometimes be seen around Birkenau. Life in the camp became 'better and better' all the time—after the first three or four years. We felt certain that the horrors could never again be repeated, and we were proud that we had survived. The worse the Germans fared at the battle front, the better off we were. And since they fared worse and worse ...

At the Persian Market, time seemed to move in reverse. Again we saw the Auschwitz of 1940. The women greedily gulped down the soup which nobody in our blocks would even think of touching. They stank of sweat and female blood. They stood at roll-call from five in the morning. When they were at last counted, it was almost nine. Then they were given cold coffee. At three in the afternoon the evening roll-call began and they were given dinner: bread with some spread. Since they did not work, they did not rate the *Zulage*, the extra work ration.

Sometimes they were driven out of the barracks in the

middle of the day for an additional roll-call. They would
line up in tight rows and march along the road, one behind
the other. The big, blonde S.S. women in leather boots
plucked from among them all the skinny ones, the ugly
ones, the big-bellied ones—and threw them inside the Eye.
The so-called Eye was a closed circle formed by the joined
hands of the barracks guards. Filled out with women, the
circle moved like a macabre dance to the camp gate, there
to become absorbed by the great, camp-wide Eye. Five
hundred, six hundred, a thousand selected women. Then
all of them started on their walk—along the two roads.

Sometimes an S.S. woman dropped in at one of the barracks. She cased the bunks, a woman looking at other
women. She asked if anyone cared to see a doctor, if anyone
was pregnant. At the hospital, she said, they would get milk
and white bread.

They scrambled out of the bunks and, swept up into the
Eye, walked to the gate—towards the little wood.

Just to pass the time of day—for there was little for
us to do at the camp—we used to spend long hours at the
Persian Market, either with the Block Elders, or sitting
under the barracks walls, or in the latrines. At the Elders'
shacks you drank tea or dozed off for an hour or two in their
beds. Sitting under the barracks wall you chatted with the
carpenters and the bricklayers. A few women were usually
hanging around, dressed in pretty little pullovers and
wearing sheer stockings. Any one of them could be had for
a piece of bright silk or a shiny trinket. Since time began,
never has there been such an easy market for female flesh!

The latrines were built for the men and the women
jointly, and were separated only by wooden boards. On
the women's side, it was crowded and noisy, on ours, quiet
and pleasantly cool inside the concrete enclosure. You sat
there by the hour conducting love dialogues with Katia,
the pretty little latrine girl. No one felt any embarrassment

or thought the set-up uncomfortable. After all, one had already seen so much ...

That was June. Day and night the people walked—along the two roads. From dawn until late at night the entire Persian Market stood at roll-call. The days were warm and sunny and the tar melted on the roofs. Then came the rains, and with them icy winds. The mornings would dawn cold and penetrating. Then the fair weather returned once again. Without interruption, the trains pulled up to the ramp and the people walked on ... Often we had to stand and wait, unable to leave for work, because they were blocking the roads. They walked slowly, in loose groups, sometimes hand in hand. Women, old men, children. As they passed just outside the barbed-wire fence they would turn their silent faces in our direction. Their eyes would fill with tears of pity and they threw bread over the fence for us to eat.

The women took the watches off their wrists and flung them at our feet, gesturing to us to take them.

At the gate, a band was playing foxtrots and tangos. The camp gazed at the passing procession. A man has only a limited number of ways in which he can express strong emotions or violent passions. He uses the same gestures as when what he feels is only petty and unimportant. He utters the same ordinary words.

'How many have gone by so far? It's been almost two months since mid-May. Counting twenty thousand per day ... around one million!'

'Eh, they couldn't have gassed that many every day. Though ... who the hell knows, with four ovens and scores of deep pits ...'

'Then count it this way: from Koszyce and Munkacz, almost 600,000. They got 'em all, no doubt about it. And from Budapest? 300,000, easily.'

'What's the difference?'

'*Ja*, but anyway, it's got to be over soon. They'll have slaughtered every single one of them.'

'There's more, don't worry.'

You shrug your shoulders and look at the road. Slowly, behind the crowd of people, walk the S.S. men, urging them with kindly smiles to move along. They explain that it is not much farther and they pat on the back a little old man who runs over to a ditch, rapidly pulls down his trousers, and wobbling in a funny way squats down. An S.S. man calls to him and points to the people disappearing round the bend. The little old man nods quickly, pulls up his trousers and, wobbling in a funny way, runs at a trot to catch up.

You snicker, amused at the sight of a man in such a big hurry to get to the gas chamber.

Later, we started working at the warehouses, spreading tar over their dripping roofs. The warehouses contained mountains of clothing, junk, and not-yet-disembowelled bundles. The treasures taken from the gassed people were piled up at random, exposed to the sun and the rain.

Every day, after lighting a fire under the bucket of tar, we went to 'organize' a snack. One of us would bring a pail of water, another a sack of dry cherries or prunes, a third some sugar. We stewed the fruit and then carried it up on the roof for those who took care of the work itself. Others fried bacon and onions and ate it with corn bread. We stole anything we could get our hands on and took it to the camp.

From the warehouse roofs you could see very clearly the flaming pits and the crematoria operating at full speed. You could see the people walk inside, undress. Then the S.S. men would quickly shut the windows and firmly tighten the screws. After a few minutes, in which we did not even have time to tar a piece of roofing board properly, they opened the windows and the side doors and aired the place out. Then came the *Sonderkommando** to drag the corpses to the burning pits. And so it went on, from morning till night—every single day.

Sometimes, after a transport had already been gassed, some late-arriving cars drove around filled with the sick. It was wasteful to gas them. They were undressed and Oberscharführer Moll either shot them with his rifle or pushed them live into a flaming trench.

Once, a car brought a young woman who had refused to part from her mother. Both were forced to undress, the mother led the way. The man who was to guide the daughter stopped, struck by the perfect beauty of her body, and in his awe and admiration he scratched his head. The woman, noticing this coarse, human gesture, relaxed. Blushing, she clutched the man's arm.

'Tell me, what will they do to me?'

'Be brave,' said the man, not withdrawing his arm.

'I am brave! Can't you see, I'm not even ashamed of you! Tell me!'

'Remember, be brave, come. I shall lead you. Just don't look.'

He took her by the hand and led her on, his other hand covering her eyes. The sizzling and the stench of the burning fat and the heat gushing out of the pit terrified her. She jerked back. But he gently bent her head forward, uncovering her back. At that moment the Oberscharführer fired, almost without aiming. The man pushed the woman into the flaming pit, and as she fell he heard her terrible, broken scream.

When the Persian Market, the gypsy camp and the F.K.L. became completely filled with the women selected from among the people from the ramp, a new camp was opened up across from the Persian Market. We called it Mexico.

* The *Sonderkommando*, a labour gang composed mostly of Jews and assigned specifically to crematorium duties.

It, too, was not yet completed, and there also they began to install shacks for the Block Elders, electricity, and windows.

Each day was just like another. People emerged from the freight cars and walked on—along both roads.

The camp inmates had problems of their own: they waited for packages and letters from home, they 'organized' for their friends and mistresses, they speculated, they schemed. Nights followed days, rains came after the dry spells.

Towards the end of the summer, the trains stopped coming. Fewer and fewer people went to the crematoria. At first, the camp seemed somehow empty and incomplete. Then everybody got used to it. Anyway, other important events were taking place: the Russian offensive, the uprising and burning of Warsaw, the transports leaving the camp every day, going West towards the unknown, towards new sickness and death; the revolt at the crematoria and the escape of a *Sonderkommando* that ended with the execution of all the escapees.

And afterwards, you were shoved from camp to camp, without a spoon, or a plate, or a piece of rag to clean yourself with.

Your memory retains only images. Today, as I think back on that last summer in Auschwitz, I can still see the endless, colourful procession of people solemnly walking—along both roads; the woman, her head bent forward, standing over the flaming pit; the big redheaded girl in the dark interior of the barracks, shouting impatiently:

'Will evil be punished? I mean in human, normal terms!'

And I can still see the Jew with bad teeth, standing beneath my high bunk every evening, lifting his face to me, asking insistently:

'Any packages today? Couldn't you sell me some eggs for Mirka? I'll pay in marks. She is so fond of eggs ... '

Auschwitz, Our Home
(A Letter)

I

So here I am, a student at the Auschwitz hospital. From the vast population of Birkenau, only ten of us were selected and sent here to be trained as medical orderlies, almost doctors. We shall be expected to know every bone in the human body, all about the circulatory system, what a peritoneum is, how to cure staphylococcus and streptococcus, how to take out an appendix, and the various symptoms of emphysema.

We shall be entrusted with a lofty mission: to nurse back to health our fellow inmates who may have the 'misfortune' to become ill, suffer from severe apathy, or feel depressed about life in general. It will be up to us—the chosen ten out of Birkenau's twenty thousand—to lower the camp's mortality rate and to raise the prisoners' morale. Or, in short, that is what we were told by the S.S. doctor upon our departure from Birkenau. He then asked each of us our age and occupation, and when I answered 'student' he raised his eyebrows in surprise.

'And what was it you studied?'

'The history of art,' I answered modestly.

He nodded, but had obviously lost interest; he got into his car and drove away.

Afterwards we marched to Auschwitz along a very beautiful road, observing some very interesting scenery en route. Then we were assigned guest quarters at one of the Auschwitz hospital blocks, and as soon as this dreary procedure was over, Staszek (you know, the one who once gave me a pair of brown trousers) and I took off for the camp; I in search of someone who might deliver this letter to you, and Staszek to the kitchens and the supply rooms to round up some food for supper—a loaf of white bread, a piece of lard and at least one sausage, since there are five of us living together.

I was, naturally, entirely unsuccessful, my serial number being over one million, whereas this place swarms with very 'old numbers' who look down their noses at million-plus fellows like me. But Staszek promised to take care of my letter through his own contacts, provided it was not too heavy. 'It must be a bore to write to a girl every day,' he told me.

So, as soon as I learn all the bones in the human body and find out what a peritoneum is, I shall let you know how to cure your skin rash and what the woman in the bunk next to yours ought to take for her fever. But I know that even if I discovered the remedy for *ulcus duodeni*, I would still be unable to get you the ordinary Wilkinson's itch ointment, because there just is none to be had at the camp. We simply used to douse our patients with mint tea, at the same time uttering certain very effective magic words, which, unfortunately, I cannot repeat.

As for lowering the camp's mortality rate: some time ago one of the 'bigwigs' in our block fell ill; he felt terrible, had a high fever, and spoke more and more of dying. Fin-

99

ally one day he called me over. I sat down on the edge of the bed.

'Wouldn't you say I was fairly well known at the camp, eh?' he asked, looking anxiously into my eyes.

'There isn't one man around who wouldn't know you … and always remember you,' I answered innocently.

'Look over there,' he said, pointing at the window.

Tall flames were shooting up in the sky beyond the forest.

'Well, you see, I want to be put away separately. Not with all the others. Not on a heap. You understand?'

'Don't worry,' I told him affectionately. 'I'll even see to it that you get your own sheet. And I can put in a good word for you with the morgue boys.'

He squeezed my hand in silence. But nothing came of it. He got well, and later sent me a piece of lard from the main camp. I use it to shine my shoes, for it happens to be made of fish oil. And so you have an example of my contribution to the lowering of the camp's mortality rate. But enough of camp talk for one day.

For almost a month now I have not had a letter from home …

II

What delightful days: no roll-call, no duties to perform. The entire camp stands at attention, but we, the lucky spectators from another planet, lean out of the window and gaze at the world. The people smile at us, we smile at the people, they call us 'Comrades from Birkenau', with a touch of pity—our lot being so miserable—and a touch of guilt—theirs being so fortunate. The view from the window is almost pastoral—not one cremo in sight. These people over here are crazy about Auschwitz. 'Auschwitz, our home …' they say with pride.

And, in truth, they have good reason to be proud. I want you to imagine what this place is like: take the dreary Pawiak, add Serbia*, multiply them by twenty-eight and plant these prisons so close together that only tiny spaces are left between them; then encircle the whole thing with a double row of barbed wire and build a concrete wall on three sides; put in paved roads in place of the mud and plant a few anaemic trees. Now lock inside fifteen thousand people who have all spent years in concentration camps, who have all suffered unbelievably and survived even the most terrible seasons, but now wear freshly pressed trousers and sway from side to side as they walk. After you had done all this you would understand why they look down with contempt and pity on their colleagues from Birkenau—where the barracks are made of wood, where there are no pavements, and where, in place of the bathhouses with hot running water, there are four crematoria.

From the orderlies' quarters, which have very white, rustic-looking walls, a cement floor, and many rows of triple-deck bunks, there is an excellent view of a 'free-world' road. Here sometimes a man will pass; sometimes a car will drive by; sometimes a horse-drawn cart; and sometimes—a lonely bicycle, probably a labourer returning home after a day's work.

In the far distance (you have no idea what a vast expanse can fit between the frames of one small window; after the war, if I survive, I would like to live in a tall building with windows facing open fields), there are some houses, and beyond them a dark-blue forest. There the earth is black and it must be damp. As in one of Staff's† sonnets—'A Walk in Springtime', remember?

Another window looks out on a birch-lined path—the

* Two Warsaw prisons.
† A Polish lyrical poet.

Birkenweg. In the evening, after the roll-call, we stroll along this path, dignified and solemn, and greet friends in passing with a discreet bow. At one of the crossings stands a road marker and a sculpture showing two men seated on a bench, whispering to each other, while a third leans over their shoulders and listens. This means: beware ... every one of your conversations is overheard, interpreted and reported to the proper authorities. In Auschwitz one man knows all there is to know about another: when he was a 'Muslim', how much he stole and through whom, the number of people he has strangled, and the number of people he has ruined. And they grin knowingly if you happen to utter a word of praise about anyone else.

Well then, imagine a Pawiak, multiplied many times, and surrounded with a double row of barbed wire. Not at all like Birkenau, with its watch-towers that really look like storks perched on their high, long legs, with search-lights at only every third post, and but a single row of barbed wire.

No, it is quite different here: there are searchlights at every other post, watch-towers on solid cement bases, a double-thick fence, plus a high concrete wall.

So we stroll along the *Birkenweg*, clean-shaven, fresh, carefree. Other prisoners stand about in small groups, linger in front of block No. 10 where behind bars and tightly boarded-up windows there are girls—experimental guinea-pigs; but mostly they gather around the 'educational' section, not because it houses a concert hall, a library, and a museum, but because up on the first floor there is the Puff. But I shall tell you about that in my next letter.

You know, it feels very strange to be writing to you, you whose face I have not seen for so long. At times I can barely remember what you look like—your image fades from my memory despite my efforts to recall it. And yet my dreams about you are incredibly vivid; they have an almost physical reality. A dream, you see, is not necessarily visual. It may be an emotional experience in which there is depth and where one feels the weight of an object and the warmth of a body ...

It is hard for me to imagine you on a prison bunk, with your hair shaved off after the typhoid fever. I see you still as I saw you the last time at the Pawiak prison: a tall, willowy young woman with sad eyes and a gentle smile. Later, at the Gestapo headquarters, you sat with your head bent low, so I could see nothing but your black hair that has now been shaven off.

And this is what has remained most vivid in my memory: this picture of you, even though I can no longer clearly recall your face. And that is why I write you such long letters—they are our evening talks, like the ones we used to have on Staryszewska Street. And that is why my letters are not sad. I have kept my spirit and I know that you have not lost yours either. Despite everything. Despite your hidden face at the Gestapo headquarters, despite the typhoid fever, despite the pneumonia—and despite the shaved head.

But the people here ... you see, they have lived through and survived all the incredible horrors of the concentration camp, the concentration camp of the early years, about which one hears so many fantastic stories. At one time they weighed sixty pounds or less, they were beaten, selected for the gas chamber—you can understand, then, why today they wear ridiculous tight jackets, walk with a characteristic sway, and have nothing but praise of Auschwitz.

We stroll along the *Birkenweg*, elegant, dressed in our civilian suits; but alas—our serial numbers are so high! And around us are nothing but one-hundred-and-three thousand, one-hundred-and-nineteen thousand ... What a pity we did not get here a little sooner! A man in prison stripes approaches us: his number is twenty-seven thousand—it almost makes your head swim! A young fellow with the glassy stare of a masturbator and the walk of a hunted animal.

'Where're you from, comrades?'

'From Birkenau, friend.'

'From Birkenau?' He examines us with a frown. 'And looking so well? Awful, awful ... How do you stand it over there?'

Witek, my skinny, tall friend and an excellent musician, pulls down his shirt cuffs.

'Unfortunately we had some trouble getting a piano, but otherwise we managed,' he retorts.

The 'old number' looks at us as though he were looking through dense fog.

'Because ... around here we're afraid of Birkenau ...'

III

Again the start of our training has been postponed, as we are awaiting the arrival of orderlies from neighbouring camps: from Janin, Jaworzyn and Buna, and from some more distant camps that are nevertheless part of Auschwitz. Meanwhile, we have had to listen to several lofty speeches made by our chief, black, dried-up little Adolf, who has recently come from Dachau and exudes *Kameradschaft*. By training orderlies, he expects to improve the camp's health, and by teaching us all about the nervous system, to reduce the mortality rate. Adolf is extremely pleasant and really out of another world. But, being a German, he fails to distinguish between reality and illusion, and is inclined to take words at their face value, as if they always represented the truth. He says *Kameraden* and thinks that such a thing is possible. Above the gates leading

to the camp, these words are inscribed on metal scrolls:
'Work makes one free.' I suppose they believe it, the S.S.
men and the German prisoners—those raised on Luther,
Fichte, Hegel, Nietzsche.

And so, for the time being we have no school. I roam
around the camp, sightseeing and making psychological
notes for myself. In fact, three of us roam together—Staszek, Witek and I. Staszek usually hangs around the kitchens
and the supply rooms, searching for men whom he has
helped in the past and who he now expects will help him.
And, sure enough, towards evening the procession begins.
Odd, suspicious-looking characters come and go, their
clean-shaven faces smiling compassionately. From the
pockets of their tightly fitted jackets they pull out a piece
of margarine, some white hospital bread, a slice of sausage,
or a few cigarettes. They set these down on the lower bunk
and disappear, as in a silent film. We divide the loot, add
to it what we have received in our packages from home, and
cook a meal on our stove with the colourful tiles.

Witek spends his time in a tireless search for a piano.
There is one large black crate in the music room, which is
located in the same block as the Puff, but playing during
work hours is forbidden, and after the roll-call the piano
is monopolized by the musicians who give symphony con-
certs every Sunday. Some day I must go to hear them.

Across from the music room we have spotted a door with
'Library' written on it, but we have heard through reliable
sources that it is for the *Reichsdeutsch* only, and contains
nothing but mystery stories. I have not been able to verify
this, for the room is always locked up as tight as a coffin.

Next door to the library is the political office, and beyond
it, to complete the 'cultural section', the museum. It
houses photographs confiscated from the prisoners' letters.
Nothing more. And what a pity—for it would have been
interesting to have on exhibit that half-cooked human

liver, a tiny nibble of which cost a Greek friend of mine twenty-five lashes across his rear-end.

But the most important place of all is one flight up. The Puff. Its windows are left slightly open at all times, even in winter. And from the windows—after roll-call—peek out pretty little heads of various shades of colour, with delicate shoulders, as white and fresh as snow, emerging from their frilly blue, pink and sea-green robes (the green is my favourite colour). Altogether there are, I am told, fifteen little heads, not counting the old Madame with the tremendous, legendary breasts, who watches over the little heads, the white shoulders, etc. . . . The Madame does not lean out of the window, but, like watchful Cerberus, officiates at the entrance to the Puff.

The Puff is for ever surrounded by a crowd of the most important citizens of the camp. For every Juliet there are at least a thousand Romeos. Hence the crowd, and the competition. The Romeos stand along the windows of the barracks across the street; they shout, wave, invite. The Camp Elder and the Camp Kapo are there, and so are the doctors from the hospital and the Kapos from the Kommandos. It is not unusual for a Juliet to have a steady admirer, and, along with promises of undying love and a blissful life together after the war, along with re-proaches and bickering, one is apt to hear exchanges of a more basic nature, concerning such particulars as soap, perfume, silk panties, or cigarettes.

But there is a great deal of loyalty among the men: they do not compete unfairly. The girls at the windows are tender and desirable, but, like goldfish in an aquarium, unattainable.

This is how the Puff looks from the outside. To get inside you need a slip of paper issued by the clerical office as a reward for good conduct and diligent work. As guests from Birkenau, we were offered priority in this regard also, but we declined the favour; let the criminals use the facilities intended for them. Forgive me, therefore, but my report must be of necessity only second-hand, although it relies on such excellent witnesses as, for example, old prisoner M from our barracks, whose serial number is almost three times lower than the last two figures in mine. One of the original founding fathers, you know! Which is why he rocks from side to side like a duck when he walks, and wears wide, carefully pressed trousers secured in front with safety pins. In the evening he returns to the barracks excited and happy. His system is to go to the clerical office when the numbers of the 'elect' are being called, waiting to see if there will be an absentee. When this happens, he shouts *hier*, snatches the pass and races over to the Madame. He slips several packets of cigarettes in her hand, undergoes a few treatments of a hygienic nature, and, all sprayed and fresh, leaps upstairs. The Juliets stroll along the narrow hallway, their fluffy robes carelessly wrapped around them. In passing, one of them may ask prisoner M indifferently:

'What number have you got?'

'Eight,' he answers, glancing at his slip to make sure.

'Ah, it's not for me, it's for Irma, the little blonde over there,' she will mutter and walks back to the window, her hips swaying softly.

Then prisoner M goes to room No. 8. Before he enters, he must read a notice on the door saying that such and such is strictly forbidden, under severe penalty, that only such and such (a detailed list follows) is allowed, but only for so many minutes. He sighs at the sight of a spy-hole, which is occasionally used for peeping by the other girls, occasionally by the Madame, or the Puff's Kommandoführer, or the camp Kommandant himself. He drops a packet of cigarettes on the table, and ... oh, at the same time he notices two packets of English cigarettes on top of the

dresser. Then he does what he has come for and departs ...
absent-mindedly slipping the English cigarettes into his
pocket. Once more he undergoes a disinfecting treatment,
and later, pleased with himself and cheerful, he relates his
adventure to us blow by blow.

But once in a while all the precautions fail ... only
recently the Puff again became contaminated. The place
was locked up, the customers, traced through their numbers, were called in and subjected to a radical treatment.
But, because of the flourishing black-market in passes, in
most cases the wrong men underwent the cure. Ha, such is
life. The Puff girls also used to make trips inside the camp.
Dressed in men's suits, they would climb down a ladder
in the middle of the night to join a drinking brawl or an
orgy of some kind. But an S.S. guard from a near-by sector
did not like it, and that was the end of that.

There is another place where women may be found:
No. 10, the experimental block. The women in No. 10 are
being artificially inseminated, injected with typhoid and
malaria germs, or operated on. I once caught a glimpse of
the man who heads the project: a man in a green hunting
outfit and a gay little Tyrolian hat decorated with many
brightly shining sports emblems, a man with the face of
a kindly satyr. A university professor, I am told.

The women are kept behind barred and boarded-up
windows, but still the place is often broken into and the
women are inseminated, not at all artificially. This must
make the old professor very angry indeed.

But you must not misunderstand—these men are not
maniacs or perverts. Every man in the camp, as soon as he
has had enough food and sleep, talks about women. Every
man in the camp dreams about women. Every man in
the camp tries to get hold of a woman. One camp Elder
wound up in a penal transport for repeatedly climbing
through the window into the Puff. A nineteen-year-old S.S.

man once caught the orchestra conductor, a stout, respectable gentleman, and several dentists inside an ambulance in unambiguous positions with the female patients who had come to have their teeth pulled. With a club which he happened to have in his hand, the young S.S. man administered due punishment across the most readily available parts of their anatomy. An episode of this sort is no discredit to anyone: you are unlucky if you are caught, that is all.

The woman obsession in the camp increases steadily. No wonder the Puff girls are treated like normal women with whom one talks of love and family. No wonder the men are so eager to visit the F.K.L. in Birkenau. And stop to think, this is true not only of Auschwitz, it is true also of hundreds of 'great' concentration camps, hundreds of *Oflags* and *Stalags* ...

Do you know what I am thinking about as I write to you?

It is late evening. Separated by a large cabinet from the rest of the huge sick-ward full of heavily breathing patients, I sit alone by a dark window which reflects my face, the green lampshade, and the white sheet of paper on the table. Franz, a young boy from Vienna, took a liking to me the very first evening he arrived—so now I am sitting at his table, under his lamp, and am writing this letter to you on his paper. But I shall not write about the subjects we were discussing today at the camp: German literature, wine, romantic philosophy, problems of materialism.

Do you know what I am thinking about?

I am thinking about Staryszewska Street. I look at the dark window, at my face reflected in the glass, and outside I see the blackness occasionally broken by the sudden flash of the watch-tower searchlight that silhouettes fragments of objects in the dark. I look into the night and I think of Staryszewska Street. I remember the sky, pale and luminous, and the bombed-out house across the street. I think of how much I longed for your body during those days, and I often smile to myself imagining the consternation after my arrest when they must have found in my room, next to my books and my poems, your perfume and your robe, heavy and red like the brocades in Velazquez's paintings.

I think of how very mature you were; what devotion and—forgive me if I say it now—selflessness you brought to our love, how graciously you used to walk into my life which offered you nothing but a single room without plumbing, evenings with cold tea, a few wilting flowers, a dog that was always playfully gnawing at your shoes, and a paraffin lamp.

I think about these things and smile condescendingly when people speak to me of morality, of law, of tradition, of obligation ... Or when they discard all tenderness and sentiment and, shaking their fists, proclaim this the age of toughness. I smile and I think that one human being must always be discovering another—through love. And that this is the most important thing on earth, and the most lasting.

And I think about my cell at the Pawiak prison. During the first week I felt I would not be able to endure a day without a book, without the circle of light under the paraffin lamp in the evening, without a sheet of paper, without you ...

And indeed, habit is a powerful force: will you believe it, I paced up and down the cell and composed poems to the rhythm of my steps. One of them I wrote down in a cellmate's copy of the Bible, but the rest—and they were poems conceived in the style of Horace—I no longer remember.

IV

Today is Sunday. In the morning we made another little sightseeing tour, took a look at the exterior of the women's experimental block (they push out their heads between the bars, just like the rabbits my father used to keep; do you remember—grey ones with one floppy ear?), and then we toured the S.K. block (in its courtyard is the famous Black Wall where mass executions used to be carried out; today such business is handled more quietly and discreetly—in the crematoria). We saw some civilians: two frightened women in fur coats and a man with tired, worried eyes. Led by an S.S. man, they were being taken to the city jail which is temporarily located in the S.K. block. The women gazed with horror at the prisoners in stripes and at the massive camp installations: the two-storey barracks, the double row of barbed wire, the concrete wall beyond it, the solid watch-towers. And they did not even know that the wall extends two yards into the ground, to prevent us from digging our way out! We smiled to cheer them up: after all, in a few weeks they will be released. Unless, of course, it is proved that they did indeed dabble in black marketeering. In that case they will go to the cremo. But they are really quite amusing, these civilians. They react to the camp as a wild boar reacts to firearms. Understanding nothing of how it functions, they look upon it as something inexplicable, almost abnormal, something beyond human endurance. Remember the horror you felt when they arrested you?

Today, having become totally familiar with the inexplicable and the abnormal; having learned to live on intimate terms with the crematoria, the itch and the tuberculosis; having understood the true meaning of wind, rain and sun, of bread and turnip soup, of work to survive, of slavery and power; having, so to say, daily broken bread with the beast—I look at these civilians with a certain indulgence, the way a scientist regards a layman, or the initiated an outsider.

Try to grasp the essence of this pattern of daily events, discarding your sense of horror and loathing and contempt, and find for it all a philosophic formula. For the gas chambers and the gold stolen from the victims, for the roll-call and for the Puff, for the frightened civilians and for the 'old numbers'.

If I had said to you as we danced together in my room in the light of the paraffin lamp: listen, take a million people, or two million, or three, kill them in such a way that no one knows about it, not even they themselves, enslave several hundred thousand more, destroy their mutual loyalty, pit man against man, and ... surely you would have thought me mad. Except that I would probably not have said these things to you, even if I had known what I know today. I would not have wanted to spoil our mood.

But this is how it is done: first just one ordinary barn, brightly whitewashed—and here they proceed to asphyxiate people. Later, four large buildings, accommodating twenty thousand at a time without any trouble. No hocus-pocus, no poison, no hypnosis. Only several men directing traffic to keep operations running smoothly, and the thousands flow along like water from an open tap. All this happens just beyond the anaemic trees of the dusty little wood. Ordinary trucks bring people, return, then bring some more. No hocus-pocus, no poison, no hypnosis.

Why is it that nobody cries out, nobody spits in their faces, nobody jumps at their throats? We doff our caps to the S.S. men returning from the little wood; if our name is called we obediently go with them to die, and—we do nothing. We starve, we are drenched by rain, we are torn from our families. What is this mystery? This strange power of one man over another? This insane passivity that cannot be overcome? Our only strength is our great number—the gas chambers cannot accommodate all of us.

Or here is another way: the spade handle across the throat—that takes care of about a hundred people daily. Or, first nettle soup and dry bread and a number tattooed on your arm, and then a young, beefy S.S. man comes around with a dirty slip of paper in his hand, and then you are put in one of those trucks … Do you know when was the last time that the 'Aryans' were selected for the gas chamber? April 4th. And do you remember when we arrived at the camp? April 29th. Do you realize what would have happened—and you with pneumonia—if we had arrived just a few months earlier?

The women who share your bunk must find my words rather surprising. 'You told us he was so cheerful. And what about this letter? It's so full of gloom!' And probably they are a little bit shocked. But I think that we should speak about all the things that are happening around us. We are not evoking evil irresponsibly or in vain, for we have now become a part of it …

Once again it is late evening after a day full of curious happenings.

In the afternoon we went to see a boxing match in the huge *Waschraum* barracks used in the old days as the starting point for transports going to the gas chamber. We were led up to the front, although the hall was packed to capacity. The large waiting-room had been turned into a boxing ring. Floodlights overhead, a real referee (an Olympic referee from Poland, in fact), boxing stars of international fame, but only Aryans—Jews are not allowed to participate. And the very same people who knock out dozens of teeth every day, or who themselves have no teeth left inside their mouths, were now enthusiastically cheering Czortek, or Walter from Hamburg, or a young boy trained at the camp who has apparently developed into a first-class fighter. The memory of No. 77, who once fought and mercilessly defeated the Germans in the ring, revenging there what the other prisoners had to endure in the field, is still very much alive. The hall was thick with cigarette smoke and the fighters knocked each other around to their heart's content. A bit unprofessionally perhaps, but with considerable perseverance.

'Just take a look at old Walter!' cried Staszek. 'At the Kommando he can strike down a 'Muslim' with one blow whenever the spirit moves him! And up here—it's already the third round and nothing happens! He's really getting a beating! Too many spectators I reckon, don't you think?'

The spectators indeed seemed to be in their seventh heaven, and there were we, seated, sure enough, in the front row, as befitted important guests.

Right after the boxing match I took in another show—I went to hear a concert. Over in Birkenau you could probably never imagine what feats of culture we are exposed to up here, just a few kilometres away from the smouldering chimneys. Just think—an orchestra playing the overture to *Tancred*, then something by Berlioz, then some Finnish dances by one of those composers with many 'a's in his name. Warsaw would not be ashamed of such music! But let me describe the whole thing from the beginning: I walked out of the boxing match, exhilarated and pleased, and immediately made way to the Puff block. The concert hall, located directly below the Puff, was crowded and noisy. People stood against the walls; the musicians, scattered throughout the room, were tuning their instruments. Over by the window—a raised platform. The kitchen Kapo (who is the orchestra conductor) mounted it; whereupon the potato peelers and cart pushers (I forgot to tell you that the orchestra members spend their days peeling potatoes and pushing carts) began to play. I sank into an empty chair between the clarinet and the bassoon and became lost in the music. Imagine—a thirty-piece orchestra in one ordinary room! Do you know what a volume of sound that can produce? The Kapo-conductor waved his arms with restraint, trying not to strike the wall, and clearly shook his fist at anyone who happened to hit a sour note, as if to warn him: 'You'll pay for it in the potato field!' The players at the far end of the room (one at the drums, the other with the viola) tried to improvise as best they could. But almost all the instruments seemed drowned out by the bassoon, maybe because I was seated right by it. An audience of fifteen (there was no room for more) listened with the air of connoisseurs and rewarded the musicians with a little scattered applause ... Somebody once called our camp *Betrugslager*—a fraud and a mockery. A little strip of lawn at the edge of the barracks, a yard resembling a village square, a sign reading 'bath', are enough to fool millions of people, to deceive them until death. A mere boxing match, a green hedge along the wall, two deutsche marks per month for the more diligent prisoners, mustard in the canteen, a weekly delousing inspection, and the *Tancred* overture suffice to deceive the world—and us. People on the outside know that, of course, life over here is terrible; but after all, perhaps it is not really so bad if there is a symphony orchestra, and boxing, and green little lawns, and blankets on the bunks ... But a bread ration that is not sufficient to keep you alive—is a mockery.

Work, during which you are not allowed to speak up, to sit down, to rest, is a mockery. And every half empty shovelful of earth that we toss on to the embankment is a mockery.

Look carefully at everything around you, and conserve your strength. For a day may come when it will be up to us to give an account of the fraud and mockery to the living—to speak up for the dead.

Not long ago, the labour Kommandos used to march in formation when returning to camp. The band played and the passing columns kept step with its beat. One day the D.A.W.* Kommando and many of the others—some ten thousand men—were ordered to stop and stood waiting at the gate. At that moment several trucks full of naked women rolled in from the F.K.L. The women stretched out their arms and pleaded:

'Save us! We are going to the gas chambers! Save us!'

And they rode slowly past us—the ten thousand silent men—and then disappeared from sight. Not one of us made a move, not one of us lifted a hand.

V

Our medical training has now been in progress for some time, but I have written little to you about it, because the attic where we work is very cold. We sit on 'organized' stools and have a tremendously good time, particularly when we can fool around with the large models of the human body. The more serious students try to learn what this is all about, but Witek and I spend most of our time hurling sponges at one another or duelling with rulers, which brings Black Adolf close to despair. He waves his arms above our heads and talks about *Kameradschaft* and about the camp in general. We retreat quietly into a corner; Witek pulls a photograph of his wife out of his pocket, and asks in a muffled tone:

'I wonder how many men he's murdered over in Dachau? Otherwise, why would he be carrying on in this way? … How would you like to strangle him? …'

* Scrap and demolition Kommando.

'Uhm ... a good-looking woman, your wife. How did you ever get her?'

'One day we went for a walk in Pruszkow*. You know how it is—everything fresh and green, narrow winding paths, woods all around. We were walking along, happy and relaxed, when all at once an S.S. dog jumped out of the bushes and came straight at us.'

'Liar! That was Pruszkow, not Auschwitz.'

'An S.S. dog, I mean it—because the house near by had been taken over by the S.S. And the cur came straight at my girl! Well, what was I to do? I shot a few slugs into his hide, I grabbed the girl and said: "Come on, Irene, we'd better get out of here!" But she did not budge an inch—just stood there, stupefied, and stared at the revolver. "Where did you get that!" I barely managed to drag her away, I could already hear voices approaching. We ran straight across the fields, like two scared rabbits. It took me some time before I was able to convince Irene that this piece of iron was indispensable in my work.'

Meanwhile another doctor had begun to lecture about the oesophagus and other such things found inside the human body, but Witek went on, unruffled:

'Once I had a fight with a friend of mine. It's got to be him or me, I thought to myself. And the same idea, I felt certain, had occurred to him. I tailed him for about three days, but always taking care that there was nobody behind me. Finally I cornered him one evening over on Chmielna Street and I let him have it, except that I missed the right spot. The next day I went around—his arm was all bandaged up and he stared at me grimly. "I've fallen down," he said.'

'And so what did you do?' I asked, finding the story rather timely.

* A wooded suburb of Warsaw.

'Nothing, because immediately after that I was locked up.'

Whether his friend had anything to do with it or not is difficult to say, but Witek nevertheless refused to let fate get the better of him. At the Pawiak prison he became washroom attendant—a kind of helper to Kronschmidt who, together with one Ukrainian, used to amuse himself torturing Jews. You remember the cellars of Pawiak; the metal floors they had down there. Well, the Jews, naked, their bodies steaming after a hot bath, were forced to crawl over them, back and forth, back and forth. And have you ever seen the soles of military boots, studded with heavy nails? Well, Kronschmidt, wearing such boots, would climb on top of a naked man and make him crawl while he rode on his back. The Aryans were not treated quite as badly, although I too crawled on the floor, but in a different section, and nobody climbed on top of me; and it was not an ordinary occurrence but rather punishment for misbehaviour. In addition, we had physical training: one hour every two days. First running around the yard, then falling to the ground and push-ups. Good, healthy exercise!

My record—seventy-six push-ups, and terrible pain in the arms until the next time. But the best exercise of all was the group game 'Air raid, take cover!' Two rows of prisoners, chests pressed against backs, hold a ladder on their shoulders, supporting it with one hand. At the call 'Air raid, take cover!' they fall to the ground, still holding the ladder on their shoulders. Whoever lets go, dies under the blows of the club. And then an S.S. man starts walking back and forth on the rungs of the ladder lying across your body. Then you must stand up and, without changing formation, fall down again.

You see, the inexplicable actually happens: you do miles of somersaults; spend hours simply rolling on the ground;

you do hundreds of squat-jumps; you stand motionless for endless days and nights; you sit for a full month inside a cement coffin—the bunker; you hang from a post or a wooden pole extended between two chairs; you jump like a frog and crawl like a snake; drink bucketfuls of water until you suffocate; you are beaten with a thousand different whips and clubs, by a thousand different men. I listen avidly to tales about prisons—unknown provincial prisons like Malkini, Suwalki, Radom, Pulawy, Lublin— about the monstrously perfected techniques for torturing man, and I find it impossible to believe that all this just sprang suddenly out of somebody's head, like Minerva out of Jove's. I find it impossible to comprehend this sudden frenzy of murder, this mounting tide of unleashed atavism ...

And another thing: death. I was told about a camp where transports of new prisoners arrived each day, dozens of people at a time. But the camp had only a certain quantity of daily food rations—I cannot recall how much, maybe enough for two, maybe three thousand—and Herr Kommandant disliked to see the prisoners starve. Each man, he felt, must receive his allotted portion. And always the camp had a few dozen men too many. So every evening a ballot, using cards or matches, was held in every block, and the following morning the losers did not go to work. At noon they were led out behind the barbed-wire fence and shot.

And in the midst of the mounting tide of atavism stand men from a different world, men who conspire in order to end conspiracies among people, men who steal so that there will be no more stealing in the world, men who kill so that people will cease to murder one another.

Witek, you see, was such a man—a man from a different world—so he became the right-hand man to Kronschmidt, the most notorious killer at the Pawiak prison. But now he sat next to me, listening to what is inside the human body and how to cure whatever ails it with home-made remedies. Later there was a small row in the classroom. The doctor turned to Staszek, the fellow who is so good at 'organizing', and asked him to repeat everything he had been taught about the liver. Staszek repeated, but incorrectly.

'What you have just said is very stupid, and furthermore you might stand up when you answer,' said the doctor.

'I'll sit if I want to,' retorted Staszek, his face reddening. 'And furthermore, you don't have to insult me, Herr Doktor.'

'Quiet, you're in a classroom!'

'Naturally you want me to keep quiet, or I might say too much about some of your activities at the camp...'

Whereupon all of us started banging against the stools, screaming 'yes! yes!' and the doctor flew out of the door. Adolf arrived, thundered for a few minutes about *Kameradschaft*, and we were sent back to our barracks—right in the middle of the digestive system. Staszek immediately rushed out in search of his friends, just in case the doctor should try to make trouble for him. But I am convinced he will not, because Staszek has powerful backing. One thing we have learned well about anatomy: at the camp you are not likely to trip if you stand on the shoulders of men who have influence. As for the doctor, many of his camp activities are common knowledge. It seems that he learned surgery experimenting with the sick. Who knows how many patients he has slashed to bits in the name of scientific research, and how many through sheer ignorance. No doubt quite a few, for the hospital is always crowded and the mortuary always full.

As you read this letter you must be thinking that I have completely forgotten the world we left behind. I go on and on about the camp, about its various aspects, trying to unravel their deeper significance, as though there were to be no future for us except right here ...

But I do remember our room. The little Thermos bottle you once bought for me. It did not fit inside my pocket, so—to your dismay—it ended up under the bed. Or the round-up of civilians at Zoliborz, the course of which you kept reporting to me all through the day on the telephone—that the Germans were dragging people out of the trolley buses but you had got off at the previous stop; that the entire block was surrounded, but you managed to escape across the fields, all the way to the Vistula. Or what you used to say to me when I complained about the war, about the inhumanity of man, and worried that we should grow up to be a generation of illiterates:

'Think of those who are in concentration camps. We are merely wasting time, while they suffer agonies.'

Much of what I once said was naïve, immature. And it seems to me now that perhaps we were not really wasting time. Despite the madness of war, we lived for a world that would be different. For a better world to come when all this is over. And perhaps even our being here is a step towards that world. Do you really think that, without the hope that such a world is possible, that the rights of man will be restored again, we could stand the concentration camp even for one day? It is that very hope that makes people go without a murmur to the gas chambers, keeps them from risking a revolt, paralyses them into numb inactivity. It is hope that breaks down family ties, makes mothers renounce their children, or wives sell their bodies for bread, or husbands kill. It is hope that compels man to hold on to one more day of life, because that day may be the day of liberation. Ah, and not even the hope for a different, better world, but simply for life, a life of peace and rest. Never before in the history of mankind has hope been stronger than man, but never also has it done so much harm

as it has in this war, in this concentration camp. We were
never taught how to give up hope, and this is why today we
perish in gas chambers.

Observe in what an original world we are living: how
many men can you find in Europe who have never killed;
or whom somebody does not wish to kill?

But still we continue to long for a world in which there
is love between men, peace, and serene deliverance from
our baser instincts. This, I suppose, is the nature of youth.

P.S.   And yet, first of all, I should like to slaughter one
or two men, just to throw off the concentration camp mentality, the effects of continual subservience, the effects of
helplessly watching others being beaten and murdered, the
effects of all this horror. I suspect, though, that I will be
marked for life. I do not know whether we shall survive,
but I like to think that one day we shall have the courage
to tell the world the whole truth and call it by its proper
name.

VI

For some days now we have had regular entertainment
at midday: a column of men marches out of the *für
Deutsche* block and, loudly singing *Morgen Nach Heimat*,
tramps round and round the camp, with the Camp Elder
in the lead, marking time with his cane.

These men are the criminals, or army 'volunteers'. Those
who are guilty of petty crimes will be shipped to the front
lines. But the fellow who butchered his wife and mother-
in-law and then let the canary out of its cage so that the
poor little creature should not be unhappy in captivity, is
the lucky one—he will remain in the camp. Meanwhile,
however, all of them are here. One happy family!

They are being taught the art of marching and are

watched for any signs that they may be developing a sense of social responsibility. As a matter of fact, they have exhibited a considerable amount of 'social' initiative and have already managed to break into the supply rooms, to steal some packages, destroy the canteen and demolish the Puff (so it is closed again, to everyone's sorrow). 'Why in hell', they say—and very wisely—'should we go and fight and risk our necks for the S.S.? ... And who is going to polish our boots out there? We're quite satisfied to stay right here! Our glorious Fatherland? It will fall to pieces without any assistance from us ... and out there, who will polish our boots, and how are we going to get pretty young boys?'

So the gang marches along the road singing 'Tomorrow we march home'. Notorious thugs, one and all: Seppel, the terror of the *Dachdecker*, who mercilessly forces you to work in rain, snow and freezing weather and shoves you off the roof if you hammer a nail in crookedly; Arno Böhm, number eight, an old-time Block Elder, Kapo and Camp Kapo, who used to kill men for selling tea in the black market and administered twenty-five lashes for every minute you were late and every word you uttered after the evening gong; he is also the man who always wrote short but touching letters, filled with love and nostalgia, to his old parents in Frankfurt. We recognize all of them: that one beat the prisoners at the D.A.W.; this one was the terror of Buna; the one next to him, the weakling, used to steal regularly and was therefore sent to the camp and put in charge of some miserable Kommando. There they go—one after the other—well-known homosexuals, alcoholics, dope addicts, sadists; and way in the back marches Kurt—well dressed, looking carefully around. He is not in step with the others, and he is not singing. After all, I thought to myself, it was he who managed to find you for me and who then carried our letters. So I raced downstairs and said to him: 'Kurt, I am sure you must be hungry. Why don't you come up—you enlisted criminal?' and I pointed at our windows. And indeed he showed up at our place in the evening, just in time for the dinner which we had cooked on our big tile stove. Kurt is very nice (it sounds odd, but I cannot think of a better word) and really knows how to tell stories. He once wanted to be a musician, but his father, a prosperous storekeeper, threw him out of the house. Kurt went to Berlin. There he met a girl, the daughter of another storekeeper, lived with her, did some writing for the sports magazines, spent a month in jail after a row with a *Stahlhelm*, and afterwards never went back to see the girl. He managed to acquire a sports car and he smuggled currency. He saw the girl once on the street, but he did not have the nerve to speak to her. Then he took trips to Yugoslavia and Austria until he was caught and put in jail. And since he already had a record (that unfortunate first month), after the jail it was the concentration camp for him and the waiting for the war to end.

It is late evening—way past roll-call. Several of us sit around the table, telling stories. Everybody here tells stories—on the way to work, returning to the camp, working in the fields and in the trucks, in the bunks at night, standing at roll-call. Stories from books and stories from life. And almost always about the world outside the barbed-wire fence. But somehow today we cannot get away from camp tales, maybe because Kurt is about to leave.

'Actually, people on the outside knew very little about the camp. Sure, we had heard about the pointless work, paving roads, for example, only to tear them up again, or the endless spreading of gravel. And, of course, about how terrible it all is. Various tales were circulated. But, to tell the truth, we weren't particularly interested in all this. We were certain of only one thing—once you got in, you didn't get out.'

'If you'd been here two years ago, the wind would have blown your ashes out of the chimney long ago,' interrupted Staszek (the one who is such an expert at 'organizing').

I shrugged. 'Maybe it would have, and maybe not. It hasn't blown yours out, so it might not have blown mine out either. You know, back in Pawiak we once had a fellow from Auschwitz.'

'Sent back for a trial, I suppose.'

'Exactly. So we started asking him questions, but he wouldn't talk, oh no. All he'd say was: "Come and you'll see for yourself. Why should I waste my breath? It would be like talking to children."'

'Were you afraid of the camp?'

'Yes, I was afraid. We left Pawiak in the morning, and were driven to the station in trucks. It's not good—the sun is behind our backs, we thought. That means the West station. Auschwitz. They loaded us quickly into the freight trains, sixty in each car, in alphabetical order. It wasn't even too crowded.'

'Were you allowed to bring some of your things?'

'Yes, I was. I took a blanket and a robe given to me by my girl, and two sheets.'

'You were a fool. You should have left them for your friends. Didn't you know they'd take everything away?'

'I suppose so, but ... And then we pulled all the nails out of one wall, tore the planks away, and started to climb out! But up on the roof they had a machine gun and promptly cut down the first three men. The fourth foolishly stuck his head out of the car and got a bullet right in the back of the neck. Immediately the train was stopped and we squeezed ourselves against the corners of the car. There were screams, curses—total hell! "Didn't I tell you not to do it?" "Cowards!" "They'll kill us all!" and swearing, but what swearing!'

'Not worse than in the woman's section?'

'No, not worse, but very strong stuff, believe me. And there I sat, under the heap of people, at the very bottom. And I thought to myself: Good, when they start shooting I won't be the first to get it. And it was good. They did shoot. They fired a series of bullets right into the heap, killed two, wounded one in the abdomen, and *los, aus,* without our belongings! Well, I thought, that's it. Now they'll finish us all off. I was a little sad about leaving the robe, since I had a Bible hidden in the pocket, and anyway, you see, it was from my girl.'

'Didn't you say the blanket too was from your girl?'

'It was. I also regretted leaving the blanket. But I couldn't take anything because they threw me down the steps. You have no idea how tremendous the world looks when you fall out of a closed, packed freight car! The sky is so high ... '

' ... and blue ... '

'Exactly, blue, and the trees smell wonderful. The forest—you want to take it in your hand! The S.S. men surrounded us on all sides, holding their automatics. They took four men aside and herded the rest of us into another car. Now we travelled one hundred and twenty of us in one car, plus three dead and one wounded. We nearly suffocated. It was so hot that water ran from the ceiling, literally. Not one tiny window, nothing, the whole car was boarded up. We shouted for air and water, but when they started shooting, we shut up instantly. Then we all collapsed on the floor and lay panting, like slaughtered cattle. I took off first one shirt, then the other. Sweat streamed down my body. My nose bled continuously. My ears hummed. I longed for Auschwitz, because it would mean air. Finally the doors were thrown open alongside a ramp, and my strength returned completely with the first whiff of fresh air. It was an April night—starlit, cool. I did not feel the cold, although the shirt I had put on was soaking wet. Someone behind me reached forward and embraced me. Through the thick, heavy darkness I could see in the distance the gleaming lights of the concentration camp. And above them flickered a nervous, reddish flame. The darkness rose up under it so that it seemed as though the flame were burning on top of a gigantic mountain. "The crematorium"—passed a whisper through the crowd.'

'How you can talk! It's evident that you're a poet...' said Witek approvingly.

'We walked to the camp carrying the dead. Behind I could hear heavy breathing and I imagined that perhaps my girl was walking behind me. From time to time there came the hollow thud of a falling blow. Just before we reached the gate somebody struck my thigh with a bayonet. It didn't hurt, only my leg became very warm. Blood was streaming down my thigh and leg. After a few steps my muscles became stiff and I began to limp. The S.S. man escorting us struck a few other men who were up front and said as we were entering the camp:

' "Here you will have a good long rest."

'That was on Thursday night. On Monday I joined a labour Kommando in Budy, several kilometres outside the camp, to carry telegraph poles. My leg hurt like the devil. It was quite a rest!'

'Big deal,' said Witek, 'the Jews travel in much worse conditions, you know. So what do you have to brag about?'

Opinions were divided as to modes of travel and as to the Jews.

'Jews... you know what the Jews are like!' said Staszek. 'Wait and see, they'll manage to run a business in any camp! Whether it's the cremo or the ghetto, every one of them will sell his own mother for a bowl of turnips! One morning our labour Kommando was waiting to leave for work, and right next to us stood the *Sonder*. Immediately I saw Moise, a former bookkeeper. He's from Mlawa, I'm

from Mlawa, you know how it is. We had palled around together and done business together—mutual confidence and
trust. "What's the trouble, Moise?" I said. "You seem out
of sorts." "I've got some new pictures of my family."
"That's good! Why should it upset you?" "Good? Hell!
I've sent my own father to the oven!" "Impossible!"
"Possible, because I have. He came with a transport, and
saw me in front of the gas chamber. I was lining up the
people. He threw his arms around me, and began kissing
me and asking, what's going to happen. He told me he
was hungry because they'd been riding for two days without any food. But right away the Kommandoführer yells
at me not to stand around, to get back to work. What was
I to do? "Go on, Father," I said, "wash yourself in the
bath-house and then we'll talk. Can't you see I'm busy
now?" So my father went on to the gas chamber. And later
I found the pictures in his coat pocket. Now tell me, what's
so good about my having the pictures?'

We laughed. 'Anyway, it's lucky they don't gas Aryans
any longer. Anything but that!'

'In the old days they did,' said one of the Auschwitz old-
timers who always seemed to join our group. 'I've been
in this block a long time and I remember a lot of things.
You wouldn't believe how many people have passed
through my hands, straight to the gas chamber—friends,
school-mates, acquaintances from my home town! By now
I have even forgotten their faces. An anonymous mass—
that's all. But one episode I will undoubtedly remember
for the rest of my life. At the time I was an ambulance
orderly. I can't say I was any too gentle when it came to
dressing wounds—there was no time for fooling around,
you know. You scraped a little at the arm, the back, or
whatever—then cotton, bandages, and out! Next! You
didn't even bother to look at the face. Nor did anyone
bother to thank you; there was nothing to thank you for.

But once, after I had dressed a phlegmon wound, all of a sudden a man said to me, pausing at the door: *"Spasibo, thank you, Herr Flager!"* The poor devil was so pale, so weak, he could barely hold himself up on his swollen legs. Later I went to visit him and took him some soup. He had the phlegmon on his right buttock, then his entire thigh became covered with running sores. He suffered horribly. He wept and spoke of his mother. "Stop it," I would say to him. "All of us have mothers, and we're not crying." I tried to console him as best I could, but he lamented that he would never go home again. But what was I able to give him? A bowl of soup, a piece of bread once in a while... I did my best to protect little Toleczka from being selected for the gas, but finally they found him and took down his name. One day I went to see him. He was feverish. "It doesn't matter that I'm going to the gas chamber," he said to me. "That's how it has to be, I reckon. But when the war is over and you get out ..." "I don't know whether I'll survive, Toleczka," I interrupted. "You will survive," he went on stubbornly, "and you will go to see my mother. There will be no borders after the war, I know, and there will be no countries, no concentration camps, and people will never kill one another. *Wied' eto poslednij boj,*" he repeated firmly. "It is our last fight, you understand?" "I understand," I told him. "You will go to my mother and tell her I died. Died so that there would be no more borders. Or wars. Or concentration camps. You will tell her?" "I'll tell her." "Memorize this: my mother lives in Dalniewostoczny County, the city of Chabrowsk, Tolstoy Street, number 24. Now repeat it." I repeated it. I went to see Block Elder Szary who still might have been able to save Toleczka. He struck me across the mouth and threw me out of his shack. Toleczka went to the gas chamber. Several months later Szary was taken out in a transport. At the moment of his departure he pleaded for a cigarette.

I tipped the men not to give him any. And they didn't. Perhaps I did a wrong thing, for he was on his way to Mauthausen to be killed. But I memorized Toleczka's mother's address: Dalniewostoczny County, the city of Chabrowsk, Tolstoy Street ... '

We were silent. Kurt, who understood nothing of what was said, wondered what was going on. Witek explained:

'We're talking about the camp and wondering whether there will be a better world some day. How about you, have you something to say about it?'

Kurt looked at us with a smile and then spoke slowly, so we should all understand:

'I have only a short tale to tell. I was in Mauthausen. Two prisoners had escaped and were caught on Christmas Eve itself. The entire camp stood at roll-call to watch them hang. The Christmas tree was lighted. Then the Lagerführer stepped forward, turned to the prisoners and barked a command:

'"*Haftlinge, Mützen ab!*"'

'We took our caps off. And then, for the traditional Christmas message, the Lagerführer spoke these words:

'"Those who behave like swine will be treated like swine. *Haftlinge, Mützen auf!*"'

'We put our caps on.

'"Dismissed!"'

'We broke up and lighted our cigarettes. We were silent. Everyone began thinking of his own problems.'

VII

If the barrack walls were suddenly to fall away, many thousands of people, packed together, squeezed tightly in their bunks, would remain suspended in mid-air. Such a sight would be more gruesome than the medieval paintings of the Last Judgment. For one of the ugliest sights to a man is that of another man sleeping on his tiny portion of the bunk, of the space which he must occupy, because he has a body—a body that has been exploited to the utmost: with a number tattooed on it to save on dog tags, with just enough sleep at night to work during the day, and just enough time to eat. And just enough food so it will not die wastefully. As for actual living, there is only one place for it—a piece of the bunk. The rest belongs to the camp, the Fatherland. But not even this small space, nor the shirt you wear, nor the spade you work with are your own. If you get sick, everything is taken away from you: your clothes, your cap, your 'organized' scarf, your handkerchief. If you die—your gold teeth, already recorded in the camp inventory, are extracted. Your body is burned and your ashes are used to fertilize the fields or fill in the ponds. Although in fact so much fat and bone is wasted in the burning, so much flesh, so much heat! But elsewhere they make soap out of people, and lampshades out of human skin, and jewellery out of the bones.

We work beneath the earth and above it, under a roof and in the rain, with the spade, the pickaxe and the crowbar. We carry huge sacks of cement, lay bricks, put down rails, spread gravel, trample the earth...We are laying the foundation for some new, monstrous civilization. Only now do I realize what price was paid for building the ancient civilizations. The Egyptian pyramids, the temples, and Greek statues—what a hideous crime they were! How much blood must have poured on to the Roman roads, the bulwarks, and the city walls. Antiquity—the tremendous concentration camp where the slave was branded on the forehead by his master, and crucified for trying to escape! Antiquity—the conspiracy of free men against slaves!

You know how much I used to like Plato. Today I realize he lied. For the things of this world are not a reflection of the ideal, but a product of human sweat, blood and hard labour. It is we who built the pyramids, hewed the marble for the temples and the rocks for the imperial roads, we who pulled the oars in the galleys and dragged wooden ploughs, while they wrote dialogues and dramas, rationalized their intrigues by appeals in the name of the Fatherland, made wars over boundaries and democracies. We were filthy and died real deaths. They were 'aesthetic' and carried on subtle debates.

There can be no beauty if it is paid for by human injustice, nor truth that passes over injustice in silence, nor moral virtue that condones it.

What does ancient history say about us? It knows the crafty slave from Terence and Plautus, it knows the people's tribunes, the brothers Gracchi, and the name of one slave—Spartacus.

They are the ones who have made history, yet the murderer—Scipio—the lawmakers—Cicero or Demosthenes—are the men remembered today. We rave over the extermination of the Etruscans, the destruction of Carthage, over treason, deceit, plunder. Roman law! Yes, today too there is a law!

If the Germans win the war, what will the world know about us? They will erect huge buildings, highways, factories, soaring monuments. Our hands will be placed under every brick, and our backs will carry the steel rails and the slabs of concrete. They will kill off our families, our sick, our aged. They will murder our children.

And we shall be forgotten, drowned out by the voices of the poets, the jurists, the philosophers, the priests. They will produce their own beauty, virtue and truth. They will produce religion.

Where Auschwitz stands today, three years ago there were villages and farms. There were rich meadows, shaded country lanes, apple orchards. There were people, no better nor worse than any other people.

And then we arrived. We drove the people out, demolished their houses, levelled the earth, kneaded it into mud. We built barracks, fences, crematoria. We brought scurvy, phlegmon and lice.

Now we work in mines and factories, and the fruit of our labour brings enormous profits to somebody.

The story of the building of Auschwitz is an interesting one. A German Company built our camp—the barracks, halls, shacks, bunks, chimneys. When the bill was presented, it turned out to be so fantastic that it stunned not only the Auschwitz officials but Berlin itself. Gentlemen— they said—it is not possible, you are making much too much profit, there must be a mistake! Regrettably— replied the Company—here are the bills. Well yes—said Berlin—but we simply cannot ... In that case, half—suggested the patriotic Company. Thirty per cent—haggled Berlin manfully, and that is what was finally agreed upon. Since then all the bills are cut accordingly. But the Company is not worried; like all German companies, it is increasing its capital. It has done fantastic business at Auschwitz and is now waiting calmly for the war to end. The same goes for the companies in plumbing, in well-drilling, in electrical appliances; for the producers of brick, cement, metal and lumber, the makers of barracks parts and striped prison suits. The same thing is true of the huge automobile company, and of the scrap demolition outfit. And of the owners of the coalmines in Myslawice, Gliwice, Janin and Jaworzna. Those of us who survive will one day demand compensation for our work. Not in money, or goods, but in hard, relentless labour.

When the patients finally fall asleep, I have time to talk with you. In the darkness, I can see your face, and although my words are full of bitterness and hatred that must be foreign to you, I know you listen carefully.

Your fate has now become a part of my own. Except that

your hands are not suited to the pickaxe and your body not accustomed to scurvy. We are bound together by our love and by the love of those who have stayed behind, those who live for us and who constitute our world. The faces of our parents, friends, the shapes of objects we left behind—these are the things we share. And even if nothing is left to us but our bodies on the hospital bunk, we shall still have our memories and our feelings.

VIII

You cannot imagine how very pleased I am!

First of all—the tall electrician. I go to him every morning with Kurt (because he is Kurt's contact), bringing along my letters to you. The electrician, a fantastically old serial number, just a bit over one thousand, loads up on sausage, sugar and lingerie, and slides a stack of letters somewhere in his shoe. The electrician is bald and has no particular sympathy for our love. The electrician frowns upon every letter I bring. The electrician declares when I want to give him some cigarettes:

'Look pal, here in Auschwitz we don't accept payment for letters! And I'll bring the reply, if I can.'

So I go to see him again in the evening. The reverse procedure takes place: the electrician reaches inside his shoe, produces a card from you, hands it to me with a bitter frown. Because the electrician has no sympathy for our love. Besides, I am sure he is very unhappy living in a bunk—that one by one-and-a-half metre cage. Since the electrician is very tall, it must be quite uncomfortable for him.

So, first of all—the tall electrician. Secondly—the wedding of the Spaniard. The Spaniard fought defending Madrid, then escaped to France and ended up at Auschwitz. He had found himself a Frenchwoman, as a Spaniard would, and had had a child by her. The child grew. The Spaniard stayed on and on behind the barbed-wire. So the Frenchwoman started clamouring for a wedding. Out goes a petition to H. himself. H. is indignant: 'Is there no *Ordnung* in the new Europe? Marry them immediately!'

So they shipped the Frenchwoman, together with the child, to the camp, hurriedly pulled the stripes off the Spaniard's back, fitted him into an elegant suit pressed personally by the Kapo in the laundry room, carefully selected a tie and matching socks from the camp's abundant supplies, and married them.

Then the newlyweds went to have their pictures taken: she with the child at her side and a bouquet of hyacinths in her arms, he standing close to her on the other side. Behind them—the orchestra *in corpore*, and behind the orchestra the S.S. man in charge of the kitchen, furious:

'I'll report this, that you're playing music during working hours instead of peeling potatoes! I've got the soup all ready, and no potatoes! I fuck all weddings!'

'Calm down ... ' some of the other 'bigwigs' tried to pacify him. 'It's orders from Berlin. We can have soup without potatoes.'

The newlyweds, meanwhile, had finished the picture-taking ceremony and were sent to a Puff suite for their wedding night. The regular Puff residents were temporarily exiled to Block 10. The following day the Frenchwoman returned to France, and the Spaniard, again in his stripes, returned to a labour Kommando.

But now everyone at the camp walks proudly, head high. 'We even have weddings in Auschwitz!'

So, first of all—the tall electrician. Secondly—the wedding of the Spaniard. And thirdly—school is almost over. The F.K.L. girls were the first to finish. We bid them farewell with a chamber music concert. They sat at the windows of Block 10 and out of our windows flowed the sounds of the saxophone, the drum, the violins. To me, the love-liest is the saxophone, as it sobs and weeps, laughs and giggles!

What a pity Slowacki* died so early, or he would most certainly have become a saxophone player.

After the women it was our turn. Everybody assembled in our attic classroom. *Lagerarzt* Rhode (the 'decent' one who makes no distinction between Jews and Aryans) came in, took a look at us and our work, said he was very pleased and quite certain that the situation in Auschwitz would greatly improve from now on, and left quickly, for the attic was cold.

All day they have been saying goodbye to us here in Auschwitz. Franz, the fellow from Vienna, gave me a last-minute lecture on the meaning of war. Stuttering a little, he spoke of the people who build, and the people who destroy. Of victory for the former and defeat for the latter; of the comrades from the Urals and London, Chicago and Calcutta, on land and sea, who are fighting for our cause. Of the future brotherhood of all creative men. Here, I thought to myself, is a messianic vision emerging out of the surrounding death and destruction—a characteristic process of the human mind. Then Franz opened the pack-age which he had just received from Vienna and we had our evening tea. Franz sang Austrian songs and I recited poems that he did not understand.

Then I was given some medicine and a few books for the road. I squeezed them inside my bundle, underneath the food. Would you believe it—the works of Angelus Silesius! So I am quite pleased, because of everything combined: the tall electrician, the Spaniard's wedding, the school being over. And in addition—I received letters from home. They had strayed a long time, but found me at last.

* A Polish romantic poet.

I had not heard a word from home for almost two months and I worried terribly. Fantastic tales have been circulating as to the conditions in Warsaw, and I had already started writing desperate letters. And then yesterday, just think, two letters! One from Staszek and one from my brother.

Staszek writes very simply, like a man who wishes to convey something straight from the heart in a foreign tongue. 'We love you and think of you,' he says, 'and we also think of Tuska, your girl. We live, we work and write.' They live, work and write, except that Andrzej has been shot and Wacek is dead.

What a pity that the two most talented men of our generation, with the most passionate desire to create, were the ones who had to die!

You probably remember how strongly I always opposed them—their imperialistic conception of an omnivorous state, their dishonest approach to society, their theories on state art, their muddled philosophy, their futile poetry, their whole style of living and their unconscious hypocrisy.

And today, separated as we are by the barrier between two worlds, the barrier which we too will cross some day, I reopen our dispute about the meaning of the world, the philosophy of living, and the nature of poetry. And today I shall still challenge their acceptance of the infectious idea of the all-powerful, aggressive state, their awe for the evil whose only defect is that it is not our own. And even today I shall challenge their unrealistic poetry, void of all human problems.

But across the barrier that divides us I can still see their faces, and I think about them, the young men of my generation; and I feel a growing emptiness around me. They went away while still so much alive, so much in the very centre of the world that they were building. I bid them farewell, my friends on the opposite side of the barricades. May they find in that other world the truths and the love that they failed to find here!

Eva, the girl who recited such beautiful poems about harmony and stars, and who used to say that 'things aren't really that bad ... ' was also shot. A void, an ever-growing void. And I had thought that all this would be limited to us. That when we return, we should be returning to a world which would not have known the horrors and the atmosphere that are killing us. That we alone had hit bottom. But it seems that they too are being taken away—out of the very centre of life.

We are as insensitive as trees, as stones. And we remain as numb as trees when they are being cut down, or stones when they are being crushed.

The other letter was from my brother. You know how affectionate Julek has always been in his letters. This time too he tells me that they are thinking of us and waiting, that they have hidden all my books and poems ...

When I return I shall find on my shelves a new little volume of my poems. 'They are your love poems,' writes my brother. I think it is somehow symbolic that our love is always tied to poetry and that the book of poems which were written for you and which you had with you at the time of your arrest is a kind of victory *in absentia*. Perhaps they were published in memory of us? But I am grateful to the friends who keep alive our poetry and our love and recognize our right to them.

Julek also writes about your mother, that she prays for us and trusts that we shall return and that we will always be together ... Do you recall what you wrote in the very first card I received from you, only a few days after arriving at the camp? You wrote that you were sick and were desperate because you felt responsible for my being thrown into the concentration camp. That had it not been for you, etc. ... Do you want to know how it really happened?

It happened this way: I was waiting for your promised telephone call from Maria's. That afternoon, as on every Wednesday, the underground school held a class at my place. I spoke, I think, about linguistics, and I think that the paraffin lamp went out.

Then again I waited for you to call. I knew you would, because you had promised. But you did not. I cannot remember if I went out to dinner. If so, then on returning I sat again by the telephone, afraid I might not hear it from the other room. I looked through some newspaper clippings and read a story by Maurois about a man who weighed human souls in order to learn how to keep them captive for ever in imperishable receptacles, and thus find a way to unite his own soul with that of his beloved for all eternity. But he only succeeded in accidentally capturing the souls of two circus clowns, whereas his own soul and the soul of the woman in question continued to float separately in space … It was getting light when I fell asleep.

In the morning as usual I went home with my briefcase and books. I had my breakfast, said I must rush off but would be back for dinner, ruffled the ears of the dog, and went to see your mother. She was worried about you. I took the trolley-bus to Maria's and on the way down looked long and intently at the trees of Lazienki Park, of which I am very fond. Then I walked up Pulawska Street. The staircase was covered with cigarette butts, and, if I remember correctly, had some traces of blood. But it may have been only my imagination. I went up and rang the doorbell, using our code. Men with revolvers in their hands opened the door.

Since then, a year has passed. But I am writing about it so that you will know I have never regretted that we are here together. It has never even occurred to me that it could be any other way. And I often think about the future. About the life we shall have, if ... About the poems I am going to write, the books we shall read together, the objects that will be around us. I know these are small things, but I think about them nevertheless.

IX

We are back. As in the old days, I went over to my block, rubbed some of the patients with mint tea and stood around for a while, a knowing expression on my face, watching the doctor operate. Then I helped myself to the last two shots of Prontisil which I am sending to you. Finally I went to see our block barber, Hank Liberfreund (a restaurant owner from Krakow), who decided that I shall certainly be the best writer among the orderlies.

Apart from that, I spent all day long snooping around the camp, carrying my letter to you. In order to reach their destination, these few pieces of paper must have a pair of feet. It is the feet that I have been hunting for. I finally located a pair—in high, red, laced-up boots. The feet, besides, wear dark glasses, have broad shoulders, and march daily to the F.K.L. to collect corpses of male infants which must be processed through our office of male statistics and our male mortuary, and examined personally by our S.D.G. Order is the essence of the universe, or, less poetically— *Ordnung muss sein!*

And so the feet march to the F.K.L. and are, for a change, fairly sympathetic. They too, they tell me, have a wife among the female prisoners, and understand how it is. They will deliver my letter free of charge. And perhaps smuggle me in too, should an opportunity arise. Actually, I feel rather in the mood for travelling, though my colleagues suggest I take along a heavy blanket and—wrap it around me where it may afford the most protection ... With my luck and resourcefulness, they figure, I am bound to be caught on the first try. I told them to go and smear themselves with Peruvian itch ointment!

I am still examining the surrounding landscape. Nothing has changed, only there is somehow even more mud. Spring is in the air. Soon people will start drowning in mud. The breezes from the forest now carry a whiff of pine, now of smoke. Cars drive by, now loaded with bundles, now with Muslims from Buna; now with dinner for the offices, now with S.S. men on their way to change the guard.

Nothing has changed. Yesterday was Sunday and we went to the camp for a delousing inspection. The barracks seem even more terrible in the winter! The dirty bunks, the black, damp earth floors, swept clean, the stale odour of human bodies. The blocks are packed with people, but there is not one louse inside. The never-ending delousing treatments have not been in vain. After the inspections, just as we started to leave, a *Sonderkommando* marched back to camp returning from the cremo. Black with smoke, looking fat and prosperous, the men were loaded down with heavy sacks. There is no limit to what they may take; anything except gold, but this is what they smuggle the most of.

Small groups of people began stealing out of the barracks, rushing over to the marching column and snatching the awaited packages from their hands. The air became filled with shouts, cursing and the sound of blows. At last the *Sonder* disappeared behind the gate leading to their quarters, which are separated from the rest of the camp by a stone wall. But it was not long before the Jews started sneaking out to trade, 'organize' and visit with friends.

I cornered one of them, an old pal from my previous Kommando. I became ill and landed at the K.B. He was 'luckier', and joined the *Sonder*, which is certainly better than swinging a pickaxe on nothing but one bowl of soup a day. He shook my hand warmly.

'Ah, it's you! Want to buy anything? If you've got some apples ... '

'No, I haven't any apples for you,' I replied affectionately. 'So, you're still alive, Abbie? And what's new with you?'

'Not much. Just gassed up a Czech transport.'

'That I know. I mean personally?'

'Personally? What sort of "personally" is there for me? The oven, the barracks, back to the oven ... Have I got anybody around here? Well, if you really want to know what "personally"—we've figured out a new way to burn people. Want to hear about it?'

I indicated polite interest.

'Well then, you take four little kids with plenty of hair on their heads, then stick the heads together and light the hair. The rest burns by itself and in no time at all the whole business is *gemacht*.'

'Congratulations,' I said drily and with very little enthusiasm.

He burst out laughing and with a strange expression looked right into my eyes.

'Listen, doctor, here in Auschwitz we must entertain ourselves in every way we can. Otherwise, who could stand it?'

And putting his hands in his pockets he walked away without saying goodbye.

But this is a monstrous lie, a grotesque lie, like the whole camp, like the whole world.

The Death of
Schillinger

Until 1943, First Sergeant Schillinger performed the
duties of Lagerführer, or chief commanding officer of
labour sector 'D' at Birkenau, which was part of the enormous complex of large and small concentration camps,
centrally administered from Auschwitz, but scattered
throughout Upper Silesia.

Schillinger was a short, stocky man. He had a full, round
face and very light blond hair, brushed flat against his head.
His eyes were blue, always slightly narrowed, his lips tight,
and his face was usually set in an impatient grimace. He
cared little about personal appearance, and I have never
heard of an incident involving his being bribed by any of
the camp 'bigwigs'.

Schillinger reigned over sector 'D' with an iron hand.
Never resting for a moment, he bicycled up and down the
camp roads, always popping up unexpectedly where he was
least wanted.

His arm could strike a blow as hard as a metal bar; he

could crack a jaw or crush the life out of a man with no apparent effort.

His vigilance was untiring. Each of his frequent visits to the other sectors of Birkenau spread panic among the women, the gypsies, or the 'aristocracy' of the *Effekten-kammer*, Birkenau's wealthiest section, where the riches taken from the gas victims were stored. He also supervised the Kommandos working within the great circle of the watch-towers, and without warning he would inspect the prisoners' suits, the Kapos' shoes, or the S.S. guards' sacks. Furthermore, he visited the crematoria regularly and liked to watch people being shoved into the gas chambers. His name was usually linked with the names of Palitsch, Kran-kenmann, and many other Auschwitz murderers who boasted that they had personally succeeded in killing with the fist, the club, or the revolver, at least ten thousand people each.

In August 1943, we heard the news that Schillinger had died suddenly in some very unusual circumstances. Various allegedly truthful but in fact conflicting versions of the incident circulated around the camp. I myself was inclined to believe the *Sonderkommando* foreman who, sitting on my bunk one afternoon while waiting for a shipment of evaporated milk to come in from the gypsy camp ware-houses, told me the following story about the death of First Sergeant Schillinger:

'On Sunday, after the midday roll-call, Schillinger came to the cremo courtyard to visit our chief. The chief was busy, as the first truckloads of the Będzin transport had just been brought over from the loading ramp.

'Surely you realize, my friend, that to unload a trans-port, to see that everyone gets undressed and then to drive them inside the gas chamber, is hard work that requires, if I may say so, a great deal of tact. Anybody knows that until the people are safely inside, with the doors bolted, you mustn't gape at their junk, or rummage through it, or much less paw the nude women. The very fact, you see, that the women are made to strip naked alongside the men is a considerable shock to the new arrivals. Therefore you work with systematic haste, emphasizing the pressure of duties which supposedly must be performed inside the false bath-houses. And, in fact, you really do have to make it snappy if you're to gas one transport and clean away the corpses before the next one arrives.'

The foreman raised himself a bit, propped a pillow under his rear-end, threw his legs over the side of the bunk, and lighting a cigarette went on:

'So, if you get the picture, my friend, we had the Będzin transport on our hands. These Jews, they knew very well what was coming. The *Sonderkommando* boys were pretty nervous too; some of them came from those parts. There have been cases of meeting relatives or friends. I myself had ... '

'I didn't know you came from around there ... Can't tell by the way you talk.'

'I once took a teacher's training course in Warsaw. About fifteen years ago, I reckon. Then I taught at the Będzin school. I had an offer to go abroad, but I didn't want to go. Family and all that. So there you are ... '

'So there you are.'

'It was a restless transport—these weren't the traders from Holland or France who only thought of how they'd start doing business with the Auschwitz rich. Our Polish Jews knew what was up. And so the whole place swarmed with S.S., and Schillinger, seeing what was going on, drew his revolver. But everything would have gone smoothly except that Schillinger had taken a fancy to a certain body—and, indeed, she had a classic figure. That's what he had come to see the chief about, I suppose. So he walked up to the woman and took her by the hand. But the naked woman bent down suddenly, scooped up a handful of gravel and threw it in his face, and when Schillinger cried out in pain and dropped his revolver, the woman snatched it up and fired several shots into his abdomen. The whole place went wild. The naked crowd turned on us, screaming. The woman fired once again, this time at the chief, wounding his face. Then the chief as well as the S.S. men made off, leaving us quite alone. But we managed, thank God. We drove them all right into the chamber with clubs, bolted the doors and called the S.S. to administer Cyclone B. After all, we've had time to acquire some experience.'

'Well, *ja*, naturally.'

'Schillinger was lying face down, clawing the dirt in pain with his fingers. We lifted him off the ground and carried him—not too gently—to a car. On the way he kept groaning through clenched teeth: *"O Gott, mein Gott, was hab' ich getan, dass ich so leiden muss?"*, which means—O God, my God, what have I done to deserve such suffering?'

'That man didn't understand even to the very end,' I said, shaking my head. 'What strange irony of fate.'

'What strange irony of fate,' repeated the foreman thoughtfully.

True, what strange irony of fate. When, shortly before the camp was evacuated, the same *Sonderkommando*, anticipating liquidation, staged a revolt in the crematoria, set fire to the buildings and, snipping the barbed-wire, ran for the open fields, several S.S. guards turned the machine guns on them and killed every one—without exception.

The Man with
the Package

Our *Schreiber* was a Jew from Lublin who came to Auschwitz an already experienced prisoner with a few years at Majdanek behind him. Finding a close friend in the *Sonderkommando* (a tremendously influential group in the camp because it had access to the riches at the crematoria), he immediately started playing sick and had no trouble at all getting into the *K.B. zwei*—our name for Birkenau's hospital section, an abbreviation of *Krankenbau II*, and there he obtained the excellent position of *Schreiber*. A *Schreiber*, instead of bending over a spade all day, or hauling sacks of cement on an empty stomach, did clerical work. He was the object of everybody's envy and his job was competed for by the 'bigwigs' who were always trying to secure good spots for their own people. A *Schreiber* escorted patients in and out of the hospital, supervised the block's roll-call, kept the patients' records, and took part indirectly in the selection of the Jews destined for the gas chamber, which in the autumn of 1943 took place approximately once every two weeks in all the sections of our camp. For a *Schreiber*, assisted by the orderlies, led the patients to the *Waschraum*, and from there they were driven at night to one of the four crematoria which at that time still operated in shifts. Then, some time in November, our *Schreiber* suddenly went down with a fever and, if I am not mistaken, a bad case of the flu, and, being the only Jew in the block, he was marked in the first selection *zur besonderen Behandlung*, that is, for the gas chamber.

Right after the selection, our senior orderly, whom we politely addressed as 'Block Elder', went to Block 14, which was occupied almost entirely by Jewish patients, to arrange for our *Schreiber* to be delivered there first, so sparing us the unpleasant duty of having to escort him separately to the *Waschraum*.

'We are transferring him to fourteen, Doctor, *verstehen*?' he said, when he returned, turning to the head doctor who sat at the table with his stethoscope hanging from his ears, carefully examining a newly arrived patient, and slowly, laboriously, writing the data on his medical card. The doctor shrugged without interrupting his work.

Our *Schreiber*, squatting in the upper bunk, was carefully tying a string around a cardboard box in which he kept his Czech boots, laced to the knee, a spoon, a knife and a pencil, as well as some bacon, a few rolls and fruit that he had received from the patients in exchange for various favours rendered. Actually this was a fairly common practice among the Jewish doctors and orderlies at the K.B., since, after all, unlike the Poles, they could not receive packages. In fact, the Poles at the K.B., though they did have help from home, also took tobacco and food from the patients.

In the bunk next to the *Schreiber*'s, an elderly major of the Polish army was playing a solitary game of chess, his thumbs over his ears; he had been kept in the hospital for almost five months, God only knows why. Below him, the nightwatchman lazily urinated into a bedpan and immediately dived back under the blanket. Coughs and wheezing could be heard from the other rooms; bacon sizzled on the little stove; it was stiflingly hot and very humid, as always towards evening.

The *Schreiber* scrambled off the bunk holding his package in his hand. The Block Elder quickly threw him a blanket and told him to put on his sandals. They left the barracks. From our window we saw that in front of No. 14 the Block Elder pulled off the *Schreiber*'s blanket, took away his sandals and patted him on the back. Then our *Schreiber*—now wearing nothing but his nightshirt that billowed out in the wind—walked into Block 14, escorted by another orderly.

It was late evening, long after the patients had received their rations, their tea and their packages, when the orderlies finally started leading the Muslims out of the block, lining them up by the door five in a row, and pulling off their blankets and sandals. The S.S. man on duty appeared and told the orderlies to form a chain by the *Waschraum* to make certain nobody escaped.

From the window we saw our *Schreiber* come out of No. 14 holding his package in his hand; he found his place in line and, urged on by the shouts of the orderlies, shuffled with the others to the bath-house.

'*Schauen Sie mal, Doktor*, look!' I called. The doctor removed his stethoscope, walked heavily to the window and put his hand on my shoulder. 'He could show a little more good sense, don't you think?' I asked.

It was turning dark outside; you could only distinguish the white nightshirts moving against the blockhouses; the men's faces looked blurred. They turned to the left and disappeared from view. I noticed that the lamps went on over the barbed-wire fence.

'He knows perfectly well—an old timer like him—' I went on, 'that within an hour or two he will go to the gas chamber, naked, without his shirt, and without his package. What an extraordinary attachment to the last bit of property! After all, he could have given it to someone. I know that I'd never ... '

'You think so, yes?' said the doctor indifferently. He took his hand off my shoulder, his jaws working as if he were sucking at a bad tooth.

'Forgive me, Doctor, but I feel certain that you too ... ' I added.

The doctor came from Berlin, had a daughter and a wife in Argentina, and he would sometimes speak of himself as *wir Preussen*, with a smile that combined the bitterness of a Jew with the pride of a former Prussian officer.

'I don't know. I don't know what I would do if I were going to the gas chamber. I might also want to take along my package.'

He turned towards me with a shy smile. I noticed that he was very tired and looked as if he had not slept for days.

'I think that even if I was being led to the oven, I would still believe that something would surely happen along the way. Holding a package would be a little like holding somebody's hand, you see.'

He turned from the window, sat down behind the table, and asked that the next patient be brought in. He was preparing a shipment of 'cureds' to be sent back to camp the following day.

The sick Jews filled the *Waschraum* with shrieks and moans, and wanted to set fire to the buildings, but not one of them dared to touch the S.S. sanitation officer who was seated in the corner with his eyes closed, either pretending to be asleep or actually sleeping. A little later, heavy crematorium trucks drove up; several S.S. men entered and told the Jews to leave everything in the *Waschraum*. Then the orderlies began to shove them naked into the trucks until they were completely packed with huge masses of people. They were driven off in the glare of the floodlights, weeping and cursing their fate and desperately holding on to each other to keep from falling off.

I do not know why, but it was said later around the camp that the Jews who were driven to the gas chamber sang some soul-stirring Hebrew song which nobody could understand.

The Supper

We waited patiently for the darkness to fall. The sun had already slipped far beyond the hills. Deepening shadows, permeated with the evening mist, lay over the freshly ploughed hillsides and valleys, still covered with occasional patches of dirty snow; but here and there, along the sagging underbelly of the sky, heavy with rain clouds, you could still see a few rose-coloured streaks of sunlight.

A dark, gusty wind, heavy with the smells of the thawing, sour earth, tossed the clouds about and cut through your body like a blade of ice. A solitary piece of tar-board, torn by a stronger gust, rattled monotonously on a rooftop; a dry but penetrating chill was moving in from the fields. In the valley below, wheels clattered against rails and locomotives whined mournfully. Dusk was falling; our hunger was growing more and more terrible; the traffic along the highway had died down almost completely, only now and then the wind would waft a fragment of conversation, a coachman's call, or the occasional rumble of a cow-drawn cart; the cows dragged their hooves lazily along the gravel. The clatter of wooden sandals on the pavement and the guttural laughter of the peasant girls hurrying to a Saturday night dance at the village were slowly fading in the distance.

The darkness thickened at last and a soft rain began to fall. Several bluish lamps, swaying to and fro on top of high lamp-posts, threw a dim light over the black, tangled tree branches reaching out over the road, the shiny sentry-shack roofs, and the empty pavement that glistened like a wet leather strap. The soldiers marched under the circle of lights and then disappeared again in the dark. The sound of their footsteps on the road were coming nearer.

And then the camp Kommandant's driver threw a searchlight beam on a passage between two blockhouses. Twenty Russian soldiers in camp stripes, their arms tied with barbed-wire behind their backs, were being led out of the washroom and driven down the embankment. The Block Elders lined them up along the pavement facing the crowd that had been standing there for many silent hours, motionless, bareheaded, hungry. In the strong glare, the Russians' bodies stood out incredibly clearly. Every fold, bulge or wrinkle in their clothing; the cracked soles in their worn-out boots; the dry lumps of brown clay stuck to the edges of their trousers; the thick seams along their crotches; the white thread showing on the blue stripe of their prison suits; their sagging buttocks; their stiff hands and bloodless fingers twisted in pain, with drops of dry blood at the joints; their swollen wrists where the skin had started turning blue from the rusty wire cutting into the flesh; their naked elbows, pulled back unnaturally and tied with another piece of wire—all this emerged out of the surrounding blackness as if carved in ice. The elongated shadows of the men fell across the road and the barbed-wire fences glittering with tiny drops of water, and were lost on the hillside covered with dry, rustling grasses.

The Kommandant, a greying, sunburned man, who had come from the village especially for the occasion, crossed the lighted area with a tired but firm step and, stopping at the edge of the darkness, decided that the two rows of Russians were indeed a proper distance apart. From then on matters proceeded quickly, though maybe not quite quickly enough for the freezing body and the empty stomach that had been waiting seventeen hours for a pint of soup, still kept hot perhaps in the kettles at the barracks. 'This is a serious matter!' cried a very young Camp Elder, stepping out from behind the Kommandant. He had one hand under the lapel of his 'Custom made', fitted black jacket, and in the other hand he was holding a willow crop which he kept tapping rhythmically against the top of his high boots.

'These men—they are criminals! I reckon I don't have to explain... They are Communists! Herr Kommandant says to tell you that they are going to be punished properly, and what the Herr Kommandant says... Well boys, I tell you, you too had better be careful, eh?'

'Los, los, we have no time to waste,' interrupted the Kommandant, turning to an officer in an unbuttoned topcoat. He was leaning against the fender of his small Skoda automobile and slowly removing his gloves.

'This certainly shouldn't take long,' said the officer in the unbuttoned top-coat. He snapped his fingers, a smile at the corner of his mouth.

'Ja, and tonight the entire camp again will go without dinner!' shouted the young Camp Elder. 'The Block Elders will carry the soup back to the kitchen and... if even one cup is missing, you'll have to answer to me. Understand, boys?'

A long, deep sigh went through the crowd. Slowly,

slowly, the rear rows began pushing forward; the crowd near the road grew denser and a pleasant warmth spread along your back from the breath of the men pressing behind you, preparing to jump forward.

The Kommandant gave a signal and out of the darkness emerged a long line of S.S. men with rifles in their hands. They placed themselves neatly behind the Russians, each behind one man. You could no longer tell that they had returned from the labour Kommandos with us. They had had time to eat, to change to fresh, gala uniforms, and even to have a manicure. Their fingers were clenched tightly around their rifle butts and their fingernails looked neat and pink; apparently they were planning to join the local girls at the village dance. They cocked their rifles sharply, leaned the rifle butts on their hips and pressed the muzzles up against the clean-shaven napes of the Russians.

'Achtung! Bereit, Feuer!' said the Kommandant without raising his voice. The rifles barked, the soldiers jumped back a step to keep from being splattered by the shattered heads. The Russians seemed to quiver on their feet for an instant and then fell to the ground like heavy sacks, splashing the pavement with blood and scattered chunks of brain. Throwing their rifles over their shoulders, the soldiers marched off quickly. The corpses were dragged temporarily under the fence. The Kommandant and his retinue got into the Skoda; it backed up to the gate, snorting loudly.

No sooner was the greying, sunburned Kommandant out of sight than the silent crowd, pressing forward more and more persistently, burst into a shrieking roar, and fell in an avalanche on the blood-spattered pavement, swarming over it noisily. Then, dispersed by the Block Elders and the barracks chiefs called in for help from the camp, they scattered and disappeared one by one inside the blocks.

I had been standing some distance away from the place of execution so I could not reach the road. But the following day, when we were again driven out to work, a 'Muslimized' Jew from Estonia who was helping me haul steel bars tried to convince me all day that human brains are, in fact, so tender you can eat them absolutely raw.

A True Story

I felt certain I was going to die. I lay on a bare straw mattress under a blanket that stank of the dried-up excrement and pus of my predecessors. I was so weak I could not even scratch myself or chase away the fleas. Enormous bedsores covered my hips, buttocks, and shoulders. My skin, stretched tightly over the bones, felt red and hot, as from fresh sunburn. Disgusted by my own body, I found relief in listening to the groans of others. At times I thought I would suffocate from thirst. Then I would part my parched lips and, daydreaming of a brimming cup of cold water, fix a blank stare on the small fragment of empty sky that stretched outside the open window. It looked like rain, for an ash-grey smoke hovered low over the roof-tops. The tar was melting on the roofs and it glistened in the sun like quicksilver.

When the raw meat of my buttocks and back started turning to fire, I would roll over to my side on the rough straw mattress, and, resting my head on my fist, gaze up anxiously at Kapo Kwasniak, the swollen man in the bed next to mine. On a stool by his side, next to a half-eaten apple and a carelessly abandoned piece of dry bread, stood a cup full of coffee. At the foot of his bed, inside a cardboard box hidden under the sheet, ripened several green tomatoes sent to him by his loving wife.

Kapo Kwasniak detested inactivity. He felt a nostalgic longing for his Kommando working in the women's section. He was bored. At the *Krankenbau* (the hospital—the famed K.B.), because of bad kidneys, he had been deprived of his only diversion—eating. His neighbour in the bed on the other side, a Jewish violinist from Holland, was dying quietly of pneumonia. That is why, whenever he heard my mattress creak, Kapo Kwasniak would unfailingly lift himself up on his elbow, his swollen little eyes squinting inquisitively.

'So at last you have had enough sleep,' he would say angrily, barely able to hide his mounting impatience. 'For heaven's sake, go on with the story. What a goddam nuisance for a healthy man to be rotting in bed like a "Muslim". Have you noticed, by the way, that it's ages since we've had a selection?'

He showed little enthusiasm for the stories of vulgar novels, adventure films, or of any kind of play. He hated all extravagant tales on the themes of romantic literature. But he would abandon himself with passion to any ridiculous, sentimental plot as long as I managed to convince him it was taken from my own life. I did in fact drag out just about all the interesting things that ever happened to me: the aunt who was serenaded every evening by her lover, a gamekeeper; the live rooster in the physics class which we locked inside a closet to spite the professor, and which refused to crow; the girl with sores on her lips, whom I always associate, due to certain experiences, with the Polish September, and so on. Moreover, I had given him detailed descriptions of my loves, deeply regretting that I had only had two. I was being honest and told him the truth in the simplest words possible, just the truth. But time passed very slowly, and my fever rose steadily, and I was becoming more and more thirsty.

'Once, when I was in jail, a young boy came to our cell. He told us a policeman brought him in, allegedly for writing on walls,' I began slowly, running my tongue over my sore lips, and related in short the story of a boy with a Bible:

The boy had brought with him a copy of the Bible which he kept reading all day long. He spoke to no one and answered our questions reluctantly, saying as few words as possible. But on the back cover of the Bible he let me write in a poem—a message to my friends on the outside. In the afternoon a young Jew was brought back to our cell after an interrogation. He looked at the boy and said that he had seen him at Gestapo headquarters. 'Why don't you admit', he added, 'that you're a Jew like myself? Don't be afraid, you're among friends.' The boy with the Bible said that he had been brought in by a policeman and that he was not a Jew. In the evening he was taken out along with a few other prisoners and was shot in the backyard.

'The boy's name, Mr Kwasniak,' I hurried on to conclude still another of my true stories, 'was Zbigniew Namokel, and, as he himself told us, he was a bank president's son.'

Kapo Kwasniak quietly leaned towards the foot of the bed and reached under the sheet. He took out a tomato and he hesitated a moment, holding it in his hand.

'This story is not taken from your own life,' he said sternly, glancing at me out of the corner of his eye. 'I've been here a little longer than you, and—do you want to know something? He was here in this hospital, that Namokel of yours. Had typhoid fever, like you. He died in the very same bed you're lying on.'

He rested comfortably against the pillow and kept bouncing the tomato from one hand to the other.

'You may have my coffee if you like; I'm not allowed to drink it anyway,' he said after a short hesitation. 'But don't tell me any more stories.'

He threw the tomato on my blanket, moved the coffee closer to me, and tipping his head to one side watched in fascination as I glued my lips to the edge of the cup.

Silence

At last they seized him inside the German barracks, just as he was about to climb over the window ledge. In absolute silence they pulled him down to the floor and panting with hate dragged him into a dark alley. Here, closely surrounded by a silent mob, they began tearing at him with greedy hands.

Suddenly from the camp gate a whispered warning was passed from one mouth to another. A company of soldiers, their bodies leaning forward, their rifles on the ready, came running down the camp's main road, weaving between the clusters of men in stripes standing in the way. The crowd scattered and vanished inside the blocks. In the packed, noisy barracks the prisoners were cooking food pilfered during the night from neighbouring farmers. In the bunks and in the passageways between them, they were grinding grain in small flour-mills, slicing meat on heavy slabs of wood, peeling potatoes and throwing the peels on to the floor. They were playing cards for stolen cigars, stirring batter for pancakes, gulping down hot soup, and lazily killing fleas. A stifling odour of sweat hung in the air, mingled with the smell of food, with smoke and with steam that liquified along the ceiling beams and fell on the men, the bunks and the food in large, heavy drops, like autumn rain.

There was a stir at the door. A young American officer with a tin helmet on his head entered the block and looked with curiosity at the bunks and the tables. He wore a freshly pressed uniform; his revolver was hanging down, strapped in an open holster that dangled against his thigh. He was assisted by the translator who wore a yellow band reading 'interpreter' on the sleeve of his civilian coat, and by the chairman of the Prisoners' Committee, dressed in a white summer coat, a pair of tuxedo trousers and tennis shoes. The men in the barracks fell silent. Leaning out of their bunks and lifting their eyes from the kettles, bowls and cups, they gazed attentively into the officer's face.

'Gentlemen,' said the officer with a friendly smile, taking off his helmet—and the interpreter proceeded at once to translate sentence after sentence—'I know, of course, that after what you have gone through and after what you have seen, you must feel a deep hate for your tormentors. But we, the soldiers of America, and you, the people of Europe, have fought so that law should prevail over lawlessness. We must show our respect for the law. I assure you that the guilty will be punished, in this camp as well as in all the others. You have already seen, for example, that the S.S. men were made to bury the dead.'

'... right, we could use the lot at the back of the hospital. A few of them are still around,' whispered one of the men in a bottom bunk.

'... or one of the pits,' whispered another. He sat straddling the bunk, his fingers firmly clutching the blanket.

'Shut up! Can't you wait a little longer? Now listen

to what the American has to say,' a third man, stretched across the foot of the same bunk, spoke in an angry whisper. The American officer was now hidden from their view behind the thick crowd gathered at the other end of the block.

'Comrades, our new Kommandant gives you his word of honour that all the criminals of the S.S. as well as among the prisoners will be punished,' said the translator. The men in the bunks broke into applause and shouts. In smiles and gestures they tried to convey their friendly approval of the young man from across the ocean.

'And so the Kommandant requests', went on the translator, his voice turning somewhat hoarse, 'that you try to be patient and do not commit lawless deeds, which may only lead to trouble, and please pass the sons of bitches over to the camp guards. How about it, men?'

The block answered with a prolonged shout. The American thanked the translator and wished the prisoners a good rest and an early reunion with their dear ones. Accompanied by a friendly hum of voices, he left the block and proceeded to the next.

Not until after he had visited all the blocks and returned with the soldiers to his headquarters did we pull our man off the bunk—where covered with blankets and half-smothered with the weight of our bodies he lay gagged, his face buried in the straw mattress—and dragged him on to the cement floor under the stove, where the entire block, grunting and growling with hatred, trampled him to death,

The January Offensive

I

I would like to tell you a short and moral story I heard from a certain Polish poet who during the first autumn after the war came to West Germany, accompanied by his wife and mistress (a philologist specializing in classical languages), to write a series of inside reports on the incredible, almost comical, melting-pot of peoples and nationalities sizzling dangerously in the very heart of Europe.

At that time West Germany was swarming with starved, frightened, suspicious, stupefied hordes of people who did not know where to turn and who were driven from town to town, from camp to camp, from barracks to barracks by young American boys, equally stupefied and equally shocked at what they had found in Europe. These boys had come like the crusaders to conquer and convert the European continent, and after they had finally settled in the occupation zones, they proceeded with dead seriousness to teach the distrustful, obstinate German bourgeoisie the democratic game of baseball and to instil in them the principles of profit-making by exchanging cigarettes, chewing gum, contraceptives and chocolate bars for cameras, gold teeth, watches and women.

Brought up worshipping success, a success to be achieved only by the daring use of one's wits, believing in equal opportunities for everyone, accustomed to judging a man's worth by the size of his income and a woman's beauty by the length of her legs, these strong, athletic, cheerful men, full of the joy of living and the expectation of great opportunities lying around the corner, these sincere, direct men with minds as clean and fresh as their uniforms, as rational as their lives, as honest as their uncomplicated world, felt an instinctive contempt for the people who had failed to hold on to their wealth, who had lost their businesses and their jobs and dropped to the very bottom of society. But their attitude towards the courteous German bourgeoisie who had managed to preserve their culture and fortunes, and towards the pretty, cheerful German girls, as kind and gentle as their sisters, was one of understanding and friendly admiration. They had no interest in politics (that part of their lives was taken care of by the American Intelligence and the German press). They felt that they had done their duty, and now they wanted to go home—partly because they felt homesick, partly because they were bored, and partly for fear of losing their jobs and missing out on their opportunities.

For us Poles in West Germany, it was therefore very difficult to break away from the carefully watched, branded mass of 'displaced persons', to move to one of the large cities, and there—after joining a Polish political organization and becoming a member of a black-market chain—to start a normal private life. It was difficult to acquire an apartment, a car, a mistress, and official travel permits, to climb up in the social hierarchy, to move around Europe as if it were our home and to feel like free men again.

After the liberation we were carefully isolated from the surrounding communities and we vegetated throughout the beautiful, sunny month of May inside the dirty, D.D.T.-sprayed barracks of Dachau. Then Negro drivers transported us to military barracks and installed us there for the summer. We spent our time lolling in the communal ward and writing articles for patriotic publications. Under the guidance of an older colleague endowed with an almost supernatural business sense, we started trading in anything we could think of and tried to devise a legal way to get out.

After two months of efforts, so macabre but so humorous that one day they deserve to be described separately, all four of us moved into a little room belonging to the energetic Polish Committee in Munich, where we established an Information Agency. Later, thanks to our concentration camp documents, three of us were able—honestly and legally—to get a comfortable four-room apartment vacated by a Nazi who was temporarily sent to stay with his relatives and who was told to leave some of his furniture and religious pictures for us.

II

At that time we longed to emigrate, and all four of us dreamed of nothing else but to escape as soon as possible from the ghetto of Europe to another continent where we could study in peace and get rich. In the meantime we were busy with the frantic search for our loved ones. One of us was looking for his wife, whom he had last seen in Pruszków when he was leaving for a concentration camp in Germany; another—a fiancée, missing from Ravensbruck; the third—a sister who had fought in the Warsaw uprising; the fourth—a girl, whom he had left pregnant in the gypsy camp when in October '44 he was taken in a transport from Birkenau to Gross-Rosen, Flossenburg and Dachau. And all four of us, seized by the general frenzy, began searching for our families, friends and acquaintances. But the newcomers from Poland, both the refugees and those on official business, were regarded by us with considerable distrust and suspicion, almost as if they carried the plague.

Those on official business were generally taken care of by the Polish Intelligence of the Holy Cross Brigade. The refugees, on the other hand, dissolved without a trace into the nameless mass of displaced persons, although occasionally one of them would surface as a local czar of butter, hosiery, coffee or postage stamps, or take over the management of an ex-Nazi firm or factory, which represented a higher degree of social advancement.

Motivated by understandable curiosity, or perhaps partly succumbing to the magic power of fame, whose aura surrounded the poet in Poland, we invited him, along with his wife and mistress (the philologist), to stay with us for a few days. At that time we were working for the Red Cross, editing, printing and mailing mile-long bulletins on missing persons—thus our apartment was empty in the morning. In the afternoons we went swimming in the river, and in the evening we were writing a book about the concentration camp.

The poet, together with his wife and mistress, rested for several days in the mahogany matrimonial bed belonging to our landlord, recovering from the hardships of his journey. (After regaining his strength, he exhibited remarkable energy and came to know extremely well every corner of the ruined city and all the intricacies of the blackmarket, and acquired first-hand knowledge of the many difficult problems confronting the multilingual masses of displaced persons.) While resting, he read from boredom a few fragments of our book and found it much too gloomy and definitely lacking in faith in mankind.

The four of us became involved in a heated discussion with the poet, his silent wife and his mistress (the philologist), by maintaining that in this war morality, national solidarity, patriotism and the ideals of freedom, justice and human dignity had all slid off man like a rotten rag. We said that there is no crime that a man will not commit in order to save himself. And, having saved himself, he will commit crimes for increasingly trivial reasons; he will commit them first out of duty, then from habit, and finally—for pleasure.

We told them with much relish all about our difficult, patient, concentration-camp existence which had taught us that the whole world is really like the concentration camp; the weak work for the strong, and if they have no strength or will to work—then let them steal, or let them die.

'The world is ruled by neither justice nor morality; crime is not punished nor virtue rewarded, one is forgotten as quickly as the other. The world is ruled by power and power is obtained with money. To work is senseless, because money cannot be obtained through work but through exploitation of others. And if we cannot exploit as much as we wish, at least let us work as little as we can. Moral duty? We believe neither in the morality of man, nor in the morality of systems. In German cities the store windows are filled with books and religious objects, but the smoke from the crematoria still hovers above the forests…

'Certainly, we might run away from the world to a desert island. But could we really? So let no one be surprised that rather than choose the life of Robinson Crusoe, we prefer to put our trust in Ford. Rather than return to nature—we vote for capitalism. Responsibility for the world? But can a man living in a world such as ours be responsible even for himself? It is not our fault that the world is bad, and we do not want to die changing it. We want to live—that is all.'

'You want to escape from Europe to look for human values?' asked the poet's mistress, the philologist.

'Above all, to save ourselves. Europe will be lost. We are living here day after day, separated only by a fragile dyke from the deluge rising around us; when it breaks through it will tear away man's freedom like a suit of clothing. But who knows what the man who will chose to defend himself may be capable of. The fire in the crematorium has been extinguished, but the smoke has not yet settled. I would not like to have our bodies used as kindling. Nor would I want to light the fires. I want to live, that is all.'

'You are right,' said the poet's mistress with a wan smile.

The poet listened to our brief debate without saying a word. He paced with long steps back and forth across the bedroom floor, nodding in agreement with us and with his mistress, and smiling like a man who has accidentally stumbled into an unfamiliar world (his analytic, visionary poetry was well known before the war for just this kind of attitude, as well as for its lengthiness). Finally at dinner—prepared by his silent, thoughtful wife and generously sprinkled with our native vodka which never fails to warm the heart of a Pole, whatever his sex, religion or political views—the poet, crushing chunks of bread between his fingers and throwing the little balls into the ashtray, told us a story which I would like to repeat here briefly.

III

In January the Soviet armies were advancing on the battle front along the Vistula river, planning to move in one 'wolf's leap' to the Oder river. The poet, along with his wife, children and mistress, found himself after the Warsaw uprising in one of the large cities of Malopolska, and he moved into the apartment of a doctor friend of his at the city hospital building. One night, a week after the campaign had started, the Soviet tank divisions, having defeated the enemy at Kielce, suddenly crossed the little river which bordered the city. Supported only by the infantry, they attacked the northern suburbs, creating panic among the Germans who were busy evacuating their officials, documents and prisoners. The fighting lasted till morning; at dawn the first Soviet infantry patrols and the first Soviet tanks appeared on the city streets.

The hospital personnel, along with the other inhabitants, watched with mixed emotions as the dirty, unshaven soldiers slowly marched westward across the city.

Then the tanks drove in and rolled fast and noisily through the narrow, winding streets, followed by the sluggish supply trucks, the mounted artillery and the kitchen trucks. Once in a while, when they were informed that some forlorn German who had not managed to escape was still hiding in a basement or a garden, the soldiers would slip quietly down from their trucks and vanish behind the house. But soon they would return, hand the prisoners over to the rear guards, and the columns would move slowly on.

At the hospital, after the initial shock and inertia, there was a great rush of activity and much confusion; the wards were being prepared for the wounded soldiers and civilians. People were busy and excited like ants in a disturbed anthill. And just then one of the nurses rushed into the head doctor's office all out of breath, and cried:

'This you will just have to handle yourself, Doctor!'

She seized him by the sleeve and pulled him out into the hall. There the surprised doctor saw a young girl seated on the floor leaning against the wall. Water was dripping from her soaking-wet uniform, forming a dirty puddle on the shining linoleum. Between her spread-out knees the girl held a Russian automatic rifle; next to her lay her army sack. She raised her pale, almost transparent face, half hidden under a Siberian fur cap, smiled with an effort at the doctor and rose heavily from the floor. Only then did they notice that she was pregnant.

'My pains have started, Doctor,' she said, picking up her rifle. 'Have you a place where one can give birth to a child?'

'We'll find something,' said the doctor, and added jokingly: 'So you'll be busy having a baby instead of marching on Berlin, eh?'

'There is time enough for everything,' the girl answered weakly.

The nurses took the girl in hand, undressed her, washed her, put her to bed in a separate room and hung her uniform out to dry.

The child was born in the morning. It was healthy and screamed so loudly it could be heard all over the hospital. The first day the girl rested quietly and gave her undivided attention to the child. But the following day she got up and started dressing. The nurse ran for the doctor, but the girl told him curtly that it was none of his business. After she had put on her uniform, she rolled the baby in a sheet, wrapped a blanket around it, and tied it gypsy-fashion on her back. She said goodbye to the doctor and the nurses, picked up her automatic and her sack, and walked down the stairs and out to the street. There she stopped the first man she saw and asked simply:

'*Kuda na Bierlin?*'

The man blinked as if he did not understand her question, but when she impatiently repeated it he pointed in the direction of the highway where uninterrupted columns of armed vehicles and people kept moving onwards. The girl thanked him with a vigorous nod and swinging her automatic over her shoulder began marching westwards with a long, steady stride.

IV

The poet finished and looked at us without smiling. But we said nothing. Then, after we had had several glasses of Polish vodka to toast the Russian girl, we all agreed that the story was obviously made up. And even if the poet really had heard about a Russian girl having a child at the city hospital, certainly a woman who joined the January Offensive carrying a child as well as a rifle was unnecessarily endangering the most important human values; she was not being humane.

'I don't know when one is really being humane,' said the poet's mistress. 'Is it better for a man locked inside the ghetto to sacrifice his life in order to make counterfeit dollars to buy armaments and make grenades from tin-cans, or is it better for him to escape from the ghetto to the "Aryan" side, to save his life and thus be able to read Pindar's *Epinicae*?'

'I admire you,' I said pouring her another glass of our native vodka. 'But we shall ignore your suggestion. We shall not make counterfeit dollars, we prefer to earn real ones. Nor produce grenades. Factories can do that.'

'Save your admiration,' said the poet's mistress and emptied her glass. 'I escaped from the ghetto and spent the entire war hiding in a friend's house inside a sofa.'

After a while she added with a slight smile:

'Yes, but I know *Epinicae* by heart.'

V

Later the poet bought a second-hand Ford, hired a chauffeur, and taking with him the addresses of our families and messages to friends, returned to Poland accompanied by his wife and mistress (the philologist).

In the spring, two of us also returned to Poland, taking our books, our suits made of American blankets, cigarettes, and bitter memories of West Germany.

One of us found and buried the body of his sister dug out of the ruins of the Warsaw uprising; he is now studying architecture and wants to rebuild Polish cities. The other married his girl who had survived the concentration camp, and he became a writer. Our leader, the holy man of capitalism, settled in Boston.

The fourth in our group sneaked across the Alps and joined the Polish army in Italy, which was eventually evacuated to the British Isles. Before we parted he asked us to look up in Warsaw the girl from Birkenau whom he had left pregnant in the gypsy camp. He had learned from her letter that the baby was born healthy and that it was saved, along with its mother and hundreds of other sick and pregnant women destined for the gas chambers, by the Russian January Offensive.

A Visit

I was walking through the night, the fifth in line. An orange flame from the burning human bodies flickered in the centre of the purple sky.

Behind me, along with the anxious, heavy shuffling of the men, I could hear the light, timid footsteps of the women (among them walked a girl who had once been mine). In the soft darkness, I held my eyes open wide. And although the fever in my bleeding thigh was spreading throughout my entire body, becoming more and more painful with every step I took, I can remember nothing about that night except what I saw with my wide-open eyes.

That night I saw a half-naked man, drenched in sweat, who fell on the loading ramp out of the cattle car in which no air was left; he drew a breath of the cool, invigorating darkness deep into his lungs, rose and staggered up to a stranger, and putting his arms around him whispered: 'Brother, brother ...'

Another man, lying on top of a steaming heap of corpses (he had been smothered in the battle for air inside the packed train), suddenly kicked with all his might at the thief who was pulling off his brand-new officer's boots, which, after all, a dead man did not need.

In the days that followed I saw men weep while working with the pickaxe, the spade, in the trucks. I saw them carry heavy rails, sacks of cement, slabs of concrete; I saw them carefully level the earth, dig dirt out of ditches, build barracks, watch-towers and crematoria. I saw them consumed by eczema, phlegmon, typhoid fever, and I saw them dying of hunger. And I saw others who amassed fortunes in diamonds, watches and gold and buried them safely in the ground. And those who made it a sport to kill as many men as they could and seduce as many women as possible.

And I have seen women who carried heavy logs, pushed carts and wheelbarrows and built dams across ponds. But there were others who would sell their bodies for a piece of bread; who could afford to buy a lover with clothing, gold and jewellery stolen from the dead. And I also saw a girl (who had once been mine) covered with running sores and with her head shaven.

And every one of the people who, because of eczema, phlegmon or typhoid fever, or simply because they were too emaciated, were taken to the gas chamber, begged the orderlies loading them into the crematorium trucks to remember what they saw. And to tell the truth about mankind to those who do not know it.

I look out of a window framed with wild ivy and I can see a burned-out house, the remnants of an old archway, with a few columns still standing, and farther on a tall linden tree in full bloom, and the sky sloping down over the river towards the line of ruins along the distant horizon.

I sit in someone else's room, among books that are not mine, and, as I write about the sky, and the men and women

I have seen, I am troubled by one persistent thought—that I have never been able to look also at myself. A certain young poet, a symbolic-realist, says with a flippant sarcasm that I have a concentration-camp mentality.

In a moment I shall put down my pen and, feeling homesick for the people I saw then, I shall wonder which one of them I should visit today: the smothered man in the officer's boots, now an electrical engineer employed by the city, or the owner of a prosperous bar, who once whispered to me: 'Brother, brother ... '

The World
of Stone

For quite some time now, like the foetus inside a womb,
a terrible knowledge had been ripening within me and
filling my soul with frightened foreboding: that the Infi-
nite Universe is inflating at incredible speed, like some
ridiculous soap bubble. I become obsessed with a miser's
piercing anxiety whenever I allow myself to think that
the Universe may be slipping out into space, like water
through cupped hands, and that, ultimately—perhaps even
today, perhaps not till tomorrow or for several light
years—it will dissolve for ever into emptiness, as though it
were made not of solid matter but only of fleeting sound.

At this point I must confess that, although since the
end of the war I very rarely force myself to polish my
shoes and almost never shake the mud off my trouser
turn-ups, that although it is a great effort for me to shave
my face, chin and neck twice weekly, and although I bite
off my fingernails in order to save time, and never, never
hunt after rare books or mistresses, thus relating the deli-

berate senselessness of my own fate to that of the Universe, I have recently begun to leave my house on hot summer afternoons to go for long, lonely strolls through the poorest districts of my city.

I enjoy inhaling deep into my lungs the stale, crumb-dry dust of the ruins. And with my head tilted slightly to the left, as is my habit, I watch the peasant women squatting near their wares against the walls of the bombed-out houses, the dirty children running between the puddles, chasing their rag-ball, and the dust-covered, sweaty workmen who from dawn till dusk hammer at trolley-bus rails along the deserted street. And I can see as distinctly as if I were looking in a mirror, the ruins, already overgrown with fresh, green grass, the peasant women, with their flour-thickened sour cream and their rancid-smelling dresses, the trolley-bus rails, the rag-ball and the children, the workers with their muscular arms and tired eyes, the street, the square and the angry babble rising above it into the restless clouds blown on by a strong wind—I can see all this suddenly float into the air and then drop, all in a tangle, right at my feet—like the broken reflection of trees and sky in a mountain stream rushing under a bridge.

Sometimes it seems to me that even my physical sensibilities have coagulated and stiffened within me like resin. In contrast to years gone by, when I observed the world with wide-open, astonished eyes, and walked along every street alert, like a young man on a parapet, I can now push through the liveliest crowd with total indifference and rub against hot female bodies without the slightest emotion, even though the girls may try to seduce me with the bareness of their knees and their oiled, intricately coiffed hair. Through half-open eyes I see with satisfaction that once again a gust of the cosmic gale has blown the crowd into the air, all the way up to the treetops, sucked the human bodies into a huge whirlpool, twisted their lips open in terror, mingled the children's rosy cheeks with the hairy chests of the men, entwined the clenched fists with strips of women's dresses, thrown snow-white thighs on the top, like foam, with hats and fragments of heads tangled in hair-like seaweed peeping from below. And I see that this weird snarl, this gigantic stew concocted out of the human crowd, flows along the street, down the gutter, and seeps into space with a loud gurgle, like water into a sewer.

No wonder then that full of irreverence bordering almost on contempt, I walk with dignity into the massive, cool building made of granite. I climb unimpressed up the marble staircase rescued from the fire and covered with a red carpet, religiously shaken out every morning by the over-tired, ever-complaining char women. I pay no attention to the newly installed windows and the freshly painted walls of the restored building. I enter with a casual air the modest but cosy little rooms occupied by people of importance and ask, perhaps a trifle too politely, for things that are perhaps too trivial, but to which nevertheless I am entitled—but which, of course, cannot keep the world from swelling and bursting like an over-ripe pomegranate, leaving behind but a handful of grey, dry ashes.

When, after a day of scorching heat, of dust and petrol fumes, a refreshing dusk falls at last, transforming the tubercular ruins into a deceptively innocent stage set fading against a darkening sky, I walk under the newly erected street lights back to my apartment which smells of fresh paint and which I bought from an agent for an exorbitant sum, not registered with any rent commission. I settle down by the window, rest my head on my palms and, lulled by the sound of the dishes which my wife is washing in the kitchen alcove, I stare at the windows of the house across the way, where the lights and the radios are being turned off one by one.

For a few last moments I strain to catch the distant street sounds: the drunken singing from the near-by tobacco shop, the shuffle of feet, the rumble of trains arriving at the station, the repeated, stubborn hammering against the rails of the nightshift men working just around the corner—and I feel a terrible disenchantment mounting within me. I push myself firmly away from the window, as though breaking a rope which has been holding me there, go up to my desk with a feeling that again I have managed to lose valuable time, pull my long-abandoned papers out of the drawer. And since today the world has not yet blown away, I take out fresh paper, arrange it neatly on the desk, and closing my eyes try to find within me a tender feeling for the workmen hammering the rails, for the peasant women with their ersatz sour cream, the trains full of merchandise, the fading sky above the ruins, for the passers-by on the street below and the newly installed windows, and even for my wife who is washing dishes in the kitchen alcove; and with a tremendous intellectual effort I attempt to grasp the true significance of the events, things and people I have seen. For I intend to write a great, immortal epic, worthy of this unchanging, difficult world chiselled out of stone.

FOR THE BEST IN PAPERBACKS, LOOK FOR THE

In every corner of the world, on every subject under the sun, Penguin represents quality and variety—the very best in publishing today.

For complete information about books available from Penguin—including Pelicans, Puffins, Peregrines, and Penguin Classics—and how to order them, write to us at the appropriate address below. Please note that for copyright reasons the selection of books varies from country to country.

In the United Kingdom: For a complete list of books available from Penguin in the U.K., please write to *Dept E.P., Penguin Books Ltd, Harmondsworth, Middlesex, UB7 0DA*.

In the United States: For a complete list of books available from Penguin in the U.S., please write to *Dept BA, Penguin*, Box 120, Bergenfield, New Jersey 07621-0120.

In Canada: For a complete list of books available from Penguin in Canada, please write to *Penguin Books Ltd, 2801 John Street, Markham, Ontario L3R 1B4*.

In Australia: For a complete list of books available from Penguin in Australia, please write to the *Marketing Department, Penguin Books Ltd, P.O. Box 257, Ringwood, Victoria 3134*.

In New Zealand: For a complete list of books available from Penguin in New Zealand, please write to the *Marketing Department, Penguin Books (NZ) Ltd, Private Bag, Takapuna, Auckland 9*.

In India: For a complete list of books available from Penguin, please write to *Penguin Overseas Ltd, 706 Eros Apartments, 56 Nehru Place, New Delhi, 110019*.

In Holland: For a complete list of books available from Penguin in Holland, please write to *Penguin Books Nederland B.V., Postbus 195, NL-1380AD Weesp, Netherlands*.

In Germany: For a complete list of books available from Penguin, please write to *Penguin Books Ltd, Friedrichstrasse 10-12, D-6000 Frankfurt Main I, Federal Republic of Germany*.

In Spain: For a complete list of books available from Penguin in Spain, please write to *Longman, Penguin España, Calle San Nicolas 15, E-28013 Madrid, Spain*.

In Japan: For a complete list of books available from Penguin in Japan, please write to *Longman Penguin Japan Co Ltd, Yamaguchi Building, 2-12-9 Kanda Jimbocho, Chiyoda-Ku, Tokyo 101, Japan*.

FOR THE BEST LITERATURE, LOOK FOR THE

☐ **THE BOOK AND THE BROTHERHOOD**
Iris Murdoch

Many years ago Gerard Hernshaw and his friends banded together to finance a political and philosophical book by a monomaniacal Marxist genius. Now opinions have changed, and support for the book comes at the price of moral indignation; the resulting disagreements lead to passion, hatred, a duel, murder, and a suicide pact. *602 pages ISBN: 0-14-010470-4* **$8.95**

☐ **GRAVITY'S RAINBOW**
Thomas Pynchon

Thomas Pynchon's classic antihero is Tyrone Slothrop, an American lieutenant in London whose body anticipates German rocket launchings. Surely one of the most important works of fiction produced in the twentieth century, *Gravity's Rainbow* is a complex and awesome novel in the great tradition of James Joyce's *Ulysses*. *768 pages ISBN: 0-14-010661-8* **$10.95**

☐ **FIFTH BUSINESS**
Robertson Davies

The first novel in the celebrated "Deptford Trilogy," which also includes *The Manticore* and *World of Wonders*, *Fifth Business* stands alone as the story of a rational man who discovers that the marvelous is only another aspect of the real. *266 pages ISBN: 0-14-004387-X* **$4.95**

☐ **WHITE NOISE**
Don DeLillo

Jack Gladney, a professor of Hitler Studies in Middle America, and his fourth wife, Babette, navigate the usual rocky passages of family life in the television age. Then, their lives are threatened by an "airborne toxic event"—a more urgent and menacing version of the "white noise" of transmissions that typically engulfs them. *326 pages ISBN: 0-14-007702-2* **$7.95**

You can find all these books at your local bookstore, or use this handy coupon for ordering:

Penguin Books By Mail
Dept. BA Box 999
Bergenfield, NJ 07621-0999

Please send me the above title(s). I am enclosing _____
(please add sales tax if appropriate and $1.50 to cover postage and handling). Send check or money order—no CODs. Please allow four weeks for shipping. We cannot ship to post office boxes or addresses outside the USA. *Prices subject to change without notice.*

Ms./Mrs./Mr. _____

Address _____

City/State _____ Zip _____

Sales tax: CA: 6.5%   NY: 8.25%   NJ: 6%   PA: 6%   TN: 5.5%

FOR THE BEST LITERATURE, LOOK FOR THE

☐ A SPORT OF NATURE
Nadine Gordimer

Hillela, Nadine Gordimer's "sport of nature," is seductive and intuitively gifted at life. Casting herself adrift from her family at seventeen, she lives among political exiles on an East African beach, marries a black revolutionary, and ultimately plays a heroic role in the overthrow of apartheid.

354 pages   ISBN: 0-14-008470-3   **$7.95**

☐ THE COUNTERLIFE
Philip Roth

By far Philip Roth's most radical work of fiction, *The Counterlife* is a book of conflicting perspectives and points of view about people living out dreams of renewal and escape. Illuminating these lives is the skeptical, enveloping intelligence of the novelist Nathan Zuckerman, who calculates the price and examines the results of his characters' struggles for a change of personal fortune.

372 pages   ISBN: 0-14-009769-4   **$4.95**

☐ THE MONKEY'S WRENCH
Primo Levi

Through the mesmerizing tales told by two characters—one, a construction worker/philosopher who has built towers and bridges in India and Alaska; the other, a writer/chemist, rigger of words and molecules—Primo Levi celebrates the joys of work and the art of storytelling.

174 pages   ISBN: 0-14-010357-0   **$6.95**

☐ IRONWEED
William Kennedy

"Riding up the winding road of Saint Agnes Cemetery in the back of the rattling old truck, Francis Phelan became aware that the dead, even more than the living, settled down in neighborhoods." So begins William Kennedy's Pulitzer-Prize winning novel about an ex-ballplayer, part-time gravedigger, and full-time drunk, whose return to the haunts of his youth arouses the ghosts of his past and present. *228 pages   ISBN: 0-14-007020-6*   **$6.95**

☐ THE COMEDIANS
Graham Greene

Set in Haiti under Duvalier's dictatorship, *The Comedians* is a story about the committed and the uncommitted. Actors with no control over their destiny, they play their parts in the foreground; experience love affairs rather than love; have enthusiasms but not faith; and if they die, they die like Mr. Jones, by accident.

288 pages   ISBN: 0-14-002766-1   **$4.95**

FOR THE BEST LITERATURE, LOOK FOR THE

☐ **HERZOG**
Saul Bellow

Winner of the National Book Award, *Herzog* is the imaginative and critically acclaimed story of Moses Herzog: joker, moaner, cuckhold, charmer, and truly an Everyman for our time.

342 pages   ISBN: 0-14-007270-5   **$6.95**

☐ **FOOLS OF FORTUNE**
William Trevor

The deeply affecting story of two cousins—one English, one Irish—brought together and then torn apart by the tide of Anglo-Irish hatred, *Fools of Fortune* presents a profound symbol of the tragic entanglements of England and Ireland in this century.   *240 pages   ISBN: 0-14-006982-8*   **$6.95**

☐ **THE SONGLINES**
Bruce Chatwin

Venturing into the desolate land of Outback Australia—along timeless paths, and among fortune hunters, redneck Australians, racist policemen, and mysterious Aboriginal holy men—Bruce Chatwin discovers a wondrous vision of man's place in the world.   *296 pages   ISBN: 0-14-009429-6*   **$7.95**

☐ **THE GUIDE: A NOVEL**
R. K. Narayan

Raju was once India's most corrupt tourist guide; now, after a peasant mistakes him for a holy man, he gradually begins to play the part. His succeeds so well that God himself intervenes to put Raju's new holiness to the test.

220 pages   ISBN: 0-14-009657-4   **$5.95**

FOR THE BEST LITERATURE, LOOK FOR THE

☐ **THE LAST SONG OF MANUEL SENDERO**
Ariel Dorfman

In an unnamed country, in a time that might be now, the son of Manuel Sendero refuses to be born, beginning a revolution where generations of the future wait for a world without victims or oppressors.

464 pages   *ISBN: 0-14-008896-2*   **$7.95**

☐ **THE BOOK OF LAUGHTER AND FORGETTING**
Milan Kundera

In this collection of stories and sketches, Kundera addresses themes including sex and love, poetry and music, sadness and the power of laughter. "*The Book of Laughter and Forgetting* calls itself a novel," writes John Leonard of *The New York Times*, "although it is part fairly tale, part literary criticism, part political tract, part musicology, part autobiography. It can call itself whatever it wants to, because the whole is genius."

240 pages   *ISBN: 0-14-009693-0*   **$6.95**

☐ **TIRRA LIRRA BY THE RIVER**
Jessica Anderson

Winner of the Miles Franklin Award, Australia's most prestigious literary prize, *Tirra Lirra by the River* is the story of a woman's seventy-year search for the place where she truly belongs. Nora Porteous's series of escapes takes her from a small Australia town to the suburbs of Sydney to London, where she seems finally to become the woman she always wanted to be.

142 pages   *ISBN: 0-14-006945-3*   **$4.95**

☐ **LOVE UNKNOWN**
A. N. Wilson

In their sweetly wild youth, Monica, Belinda, and Richeldis shared a bachelor-girl flat and became friends for life. Now, twenty years later, A. N. Wilson charts the intersecting lives of the three women through the perilous waters of love, marriage, and adultery in this wry and moving modern comedy of manners.

202 pages   *ISBN: 0-14-010190-X*   **$6.95**

☐ **THE WELL**
Elizabeth Jolley

Against the stark beauty of the Australian farmlands, Elizabeth Jolley portrays an eccentric, affectionate relationship between the two women—Hester, a lonely spinster, and Katherine, a young orphan. Their pleasant, satisfyingly simple life is nearly perfect until a dark stranger invades their world in a most horrifying way.

176 pages   *ISBN: 0-14-008901-2*   **$6.95**

FOR THE BEST LITERATURE, LOOK FOR THE

☐ **VOSS**
Patrick White

Set in nineteenth-century Australia, *Voss* is the story of the secret passion between an explorer and a young orphan. From the careful delineation of Victorian society to the stark narrative of adventure in the Australian desert, Patrick White's novel is one of extraordinary power and virtuosity. White won the Nobel Prize for Literature in 1973.

448 pages   ISBN: 0-14-001438-1   **$7.95**

☐ **STONES FOR IBARRA**
Harriet Doerr

An American couple, the only foreigners in the Mexican village of Ibarra, have come to reopen a long-dormant copper mine. Their plan is to live out their lives here, connected to the place and to each other. Along the way, they learn much about life, death, and the tide of fate from the Mexican people around them.

214 pages   ISBN: 0-14-007562-3   **$6.95**

FOR THE BEST IN PAPERBACKS, LOOK FOR THE

Also available from King Penguin:

☐ **THE DEPTFORD TRILOGY**
Robertson Davies

A glittering, fantastical, cunningly contrived trilogy of novels that centers on the mystery "Who killed Boy Staunton?," *Fifth Business, The Manticore,* and *World of Wonders* lure the reader through a labyrinth of myth, history, and magic.

"[Davies] conveys a sense of real life lived in a fully imagined . . . world."
— *New York Times Book Review*

864 pages   ISBN: 0-14-006500-8 $8.95

☐ **THE MONKEY'S WRENCH**
Primo Levi

Through the mesmerizing tales told by two characters—one, a construction worker/philosopher who has built towers and bridges in India and Alaska; the other, a writer/chemist, rigger of words and molecules—Primo Levi celebrates the joys of work and the art of storytelling.

"A further extension of Levi's remarkable sensibility, his survivor's sense of will . . . and his sense of humor" — *Washington Post Book World*

174 pages   ISBN: 0-14-010357-0 $6.95

☐ **THE PROGRESS OF LOVE**
Alice Munro

Hailed by *The New York Times Book Review* as "one of the best books of 1986," these eleven short stories feature characters who struggle in a brutal yet mysteriously beautiful world, telling us much about ourselves, our choices, and our experiences of love.

"Alice Munro is a born teller of tales." — *The Washington Post*

310 pages   ISBN: 0-14-010553-0 $6.95

You can find all these books at your local bookstore, or use this handy coupon for ordering:

Penguin Books By Mail
Dept. BA Box 999
Bergenfield, NJ 07621-0999

Please send me the above title(s). I am enclosing _____
(please add sales tax if appropriate and $1.50 to cover postage and handling). Send check or money order—no CODs. Please allow four weeks for shipping. We cannot ship to post office boxes or addresses outside the USA. *Prices subject to change without notice.*

Ms./Mrs./Mr. _____

Address _____

City/State _____ Zip _____

Sales tax: CA: 6.5%   NY: 8.25%   NJ: 6%   PA: 6%   TN: 5.5%

☐ **THE ELIZABETH STORIES**
Isabel Huggan

Smart, stubborn, shy, and giving, Elizabeth discovers all the miseries, and some of the wonders, of childhood. These delightful stories, showing her steely determination throughout a series of disasters and misunderstandings, remind us that if growing up is hard, it can also be hilarious.

"Twists and rings in the mind like a particularly satisfying and disruptive novel"
— *The New York Times Book Review*
                                        184 pages   *ISBN: 0-14-010199-3*   **$6.95**

☐ **FOE**
J. M. Coetzee

In this brilliant reshaping of Defoe's classic tale of Robinson Crusoe and his mute slave Friday, J. M. Coetzee explores the relationships between speech and silence, master and slave, sanity and madness.

"Marvelous intricacy and almost overwhelming power . . . *Foe* is a small miracle of a book." — *Washington Post Book World*
                                        158 pages   *ISBN: 0-14-009623-X*   **$6.95**

☐ **1982 JANINE**
Alasdair Gray

Set inside the head of an aging, divorced, insomniac supervisor of security installations who hits the bottle in the bedroom of a small Scottish hotel, *1982 Janine* is a sadomasochistic, fetishistic fantasy.

"*1982 Janine* has a verbal energy, an intensity of vision that has mostly been missing from the English novel since D. H. Lawrence."
— *The New York Times*
                                        346 pages   *ISBN: 0-14-007110-5*   **$6.95**

☐ **THE BAY OF NOON**
Shirley Hazzard

An Englishwoman working in Naples, young Jenny has no friends, only a letter of introduction—a letter that leads her to a beautiful writer, a famous Roman film director, a Scottish marine biologist, and ultimately to a new life.

"Drawn so perfectly that it seems to breathe"
— *The New York Times Book Review*
                                        154 pages   *ISBN: 0-14-010450-X*   **$6.95**

☐ **THE WELL**
Elizabeth Jolley

Against the stark beauty of the Australian farmlands, Elizabeth Jolley paints the portrait of an eccentric, affectionate relationship between two women—Hester, a lonely spinster, and Katherine, a young orphan. Their simple, satisfyingly pleasant life is nearly perfect until a dark stranger invades their world in a most horrifying way.

"An exquisite story . . . Jolley [has] a wonderful ear, [and] an elegant and compassionate voice." — *The New York Times Book Review*
                                        176 pages   *ISBN: 0-14-008901-2*   **$6.95**

FOR THE BEST IN PAPERBACKS, LOOK FOR THE

☐ **THE NEWS FROM IRELAND**
William Trevor

This major collection of short stories once again shows Trevor's extraordinary power. In the title story, his evocation of the anguished relations of an Anglo-Irish family through several generations approaches the dramatic and forceful effect of a full novel.

"Trevor is perhaps the finest short story writer in the English language." — *Vanity Fair*   286 pages   ISBN: 0-14-008857-1   **$6.95**

☐ **THE SHRAPNEL ACADEMY**
Fay Weldon

At a military school named for the inventor of the exploding cannonball, perhaps it should come as no surprise when the annual Eve-of-Waterloo dinner, for which the guest list includes a young weapons salesman and a reporter for a feminist newspaper, hilariously and spontaneously combusts.

"This is Fay Weldon's funniest novel . . . an original, unconventional comedy."
— *San Francisco Chronicle*
                    186 pages   ISBN: 0-14-009746-5   **$6.95**

☐ **SAINTS AND STRANGERS**
Angela Carter

In eight dazzling, spellbinding stories, Angela Carter draws on familiar themes and tales—Peter and the Wolf, Lizzie Borden, *A Midsummer Night's Dream*—and transforms them into enchanting, sophisticated, and often erotic reading for modern adults.

"Whimsical, mischievous, and able to work magic . . . Carter's stories disorient and delight." — *Philadelphia Inquirer*
                    126 pages   ISBN: 0-14-008973-X   **$5.95**

☐ **IN THE SKIN OF A LION**
Michael Ondaatje

Through intensely visual images and surreal, dreamlike episodes, Michael Ondaatje spins a powerful tale of fabulous adventure and exquisite sensuality set against the bridges, waterways, and tunnels of 1920s Toronto.

"A brilliantly imaginative blend of history, lore, passion, and poetry" — Russell Banks   244 pages   ISBN: 0-14-011309-6   **$7.95**

☐ **THE GUIDE: A NOVEL**
R. K. Narayan

Raju was once India's most corrupt tourist guide; now, after a peasant mistakes him for a holy man, he gradually begins to play the part. He succeeds so well that God himself intervenes to put Raju's new holiness to the test.

"A brilliant accomplishment" — *The New York Times Book Review*
                    220 pages   ISBN: 0-14-009657-4   **$5.95**